BEYOND THE STEEL WALL

ROBERT W. CELY

A Tale of Discovery

BEYOND THE STEEL WALL

ROBERT W. CELY

A Tale of Discovery
Published by Athanatos Publishing Group

Beyond the Steel Wall: A Tale of Discovery
by Robert W. Cely

Copyright Robert W. Cely, 2014. All Rights Reserved.

Published by Athanatos Publishing Group
www.athanatosministries.org

Book website:
www.beyondthesteelwall.com

ISBN 978-1-936830-61-9
Ebook ISBN: 978-1-936830-62-6

To Michelle
and to life beyond
the wall
at my

Part I

In an age when the world had grown old, an age much like our own, and like many old things it was frightened, and it was frightened because it was comfortable, because in comfort the only thing to be scared of is that you might lose your comfortable things; in this old and frightened age there was a young man who left home in search of adventure.

Unbeknownst to this young man, and much to his misfortune, there was no more adventure in the world. You see, when a world has grown old it no longer has any business with adventure, because it is much too scared to dare the unknown road. Now, it wasn't just the old men of this old age that did not dare, for that is somewhat natural for men of elder years to have left their adventures behind them, but the young men neither thought of nor thirsted for mysterious things beyond their own pale borders.

There were so many wonderful distractions for these young men in this old age, the kind that drain all the hunger and daring right out of him. Every night the city glistened with excitement, full of sports and strong drink and music that pulsed and thumped in smoke and dim lights. There were all sorts of entertainment and endless games. People danced, watched shows that thrilled them and made them laugh, and almost every night the sky exploded with fireworks, dancing in colors high above their heads.

Above all of these games and distractions were the women. For nothing can seduce the heart of a young man more than the magic of a beautiful woman. And in this age all the women were beautiful, either naturally or through the crafty hand of a surgeon who would cut and carve the ugly women up until they were as gorgeous as any other. Unfortunately, this meant most of the women looked alike. But they were very free with their sensual pleasures so there was hardly a young man who couldn't find enjoyment in the arms of a beautiful woman during his escapades in the city.

All of this meant that the world had become entertaining

and fun and full of pleasure. But there was no adventure.

Now our young man, Alistair was his name, being a product of his age did not know that he wanted adventure. Only his heart would not give him rest. Day and night he stirred and could find no contentment. All day long he would dream as he worked. It was easy to dream as he worked because he was a card puncher. Plastic or steel cards came drifting by on a belt and he would punch marks in them. His left hand held the plastic punch, his right hand the steel. All day long he punched the cards. He didn't know what they were for or why he punched them, but it was his job, so everyday he punched cards.

The Board of Labor had long ago mistaken Alistair for a simpleton, so they gave him a simple job. What they didn't know was that Alistair was a dreamer. It is not uncommon for dreamers to be mistaken with simpletons. Men who know nothing of dreams cannot see into a dreamer's heart. All he can see is a man who stares out at nothing and talks about things that no one else can see.

As Alistair worked he dreamed, though he didn't know of what. The factory buzzed around him, the clang of machinery and the hum of gears, and Alistair's heart longed for a place that wasn't the factory. He wanted to be in a place that was not the city. The closest place he could think of was the little park in the heart of the city. When he dreamed, he wanted something like the park, something like the gentle trees and the soft grass, but it wasn't the park he wanted either.

On several occasions Alistair tried to find his adventure in the city. He attended all the newest shows and got as close to the fireworks as he could, until his body vibrated with the colorful explosions, but this was not the adventure he wanted. He went deeper into the city for all the wayward clubs and party houses, where the music was stranger and the lights darker until he could barely see. But this was not what he dreamed of.

Alistair saved his money and hired an entertainment consultant. He was taken to parties at the top of towers and bedded women of exotic shape, opened his mouth to costly drugs and even jumped from the towers along a zip line. It filled him with exhilaration while he fell, but after being on the ground for an hour he longed for the dreaming place again.

Finally Alistair set to wandering the city, looking for a place that held adventure. But the world had become so safe that there was no place that held any risk at all. And though risk may also threaten us with danger, there is no adventure without risk.

One day Alistair walked all the way until there was no room to walk anymore. An ugly metal wall rose up and blocked his path. There was a door in the wall, the sidewalk edged right up to it, but the door was locked, and as much as Alistair rattled on the door it would not open.

Eventually, the rattling of the door brought the attention of the guard.

"You can't go through that door," the guard gruffly told him.

"Why not?" Alistair asked.

"I don't know," the guard said. "All I know is that you are not supposed to go through that door."

"Says who?"

"Says I, and I'm the guard. It's my job to guard this wall and make sure nobody goes out."

"Do you know what is behind the door?" Alistair asked.

"Nobody knows. I only know that I must make sure that nobody goes behind it."

Alistair went away disappointed. That night he dreamt of the door. In the dream he pushed it open and behind it lay... The dream always ended before he saw behind the door. He must have had the dream a dozen times that night, all ending just as he opened the door.

Something changed in Alistair just knowing the door was there. During the day when he punched cards his daydreams were no longer lingering and vague. He dreamt of the door. He obsessed about the door. Almost all of his waking hours he spent speculating and wondering about the door and what might lie behind it.

Because of the door Alistair lost interest in almost everything he had done before. No longer did he spend his nights in the city, spinning through the exotic clubs and endless pleasures the metropolis offered. Instead, he walked the streets, sometimes all night long, or lay in his bed thinking about the door.

He began to notice the grimness of the city around him. The austerity of the cold steel walls and grey concrete filled him with loathing. He hated the sound of the factory machinery at work. In fact, the only thing he felt he could bear was the small corner of park that he began to frequent more and more often.

At least once a week Alistair returned to the door. Every time he visited the door the same guard was there to tell him he could not pass through. Walking around beside the high, dirty steel wall Alistair found at least four other doors, just like the first. Also like the first they were all guarded by men who did not know what lay on the other side, only that the door was a border never to be crossed.

Usually, Alistair returned to the same door, the one he had discovered first. It burned in his mind too much for him to leave alone. Eventually, he became friends with the guard. In fact, the two became the best friends in the entire city. For up until that time no two people had an experience to share as Alistair and the guard did, and it needs experiences like these to form true friendships.

The guard's name was Railing. Like Alistair, the Labor Board believed that Railing was a simpleton and therefore needed a simple job. While Railing wasn't a simpleton, he wasn't a dreamer like Alistair.

In another age Railing would have been a great outdoorsman. He longed for something bigger than the small walls of the city. He came alive under the sky. But whenever they tested him it was always surrounded by walls, and all Railing could think about was how great it would be to get outside again. His spirit was the type that needed wide open spaces. And since Railing was big and naturally strong, but also seemed to have no talent for sports, it seemed fitting to make him a guard.

Everyday that Alistair would visit the two would begin by talking about the wall. Eventually, they speculated about what might be behind the door. And as they speculated, something new happened. They began to imagine what secrets might be hidden there.

"Perhaps there is great treasure," Alistair once figured.

"Maybe there is a ferocious beast that would immediately devour us," Railing suggested.

"I bet there is a bigger city, much nicer than our own," Alistair imagined aloud.

"I think it must be a stairway that leads you to the top of the sky," Railing offered.

The talk would move from the door to each other. They found out they had so much in common. Both young men hated their lives, they hated the city. Both of them had awful memories growing up, both wishing their parents had shown them more love. And most importantly, they both wished that there was something more to their lives than what it was.

It should come as no surprise that one day Alistair had a revolutionary idea concerning the door.

"What if you got the key and we opened the door to see what lay beyond?" Alistair suggested to his friend.

The mere thought frightened Railing, but thrilled him at

the same time.

"We could never do that," he whispered. "It is forbidden."

"But who would know?" Alistair argued. "You are the guard. You could get the key and no one would know."

Railing wouldn't discuss the door any further. But his mind wouldn't drop the subject either. Being as he was near the door all day long, it really was impossible for him to stop thinking of it. Day by day Alistair's suggestion wore him down. He even found the key in the office, forgotten and covered in dust. One day he took it and put it in his pocket, waiting to see if anyone noticed. A whole week passed by and no one said a word about the missing key.

The next time Alistair came to the door Railing showed him the key. His hands trembled as his new friend reached out to take it. Railing snatched the key back.

"I'm the guard," he said. "I should be the one to do it."

Together they approached the door, almost reverently. Railing slid the key in, had to force it because it had been unused for so long. It took a few tries to turn the rusted lock, but Railing was able to move the tumblers. He looked at his friend who nodded his encouragement and with a groan forced the door open.

Now it was night when the friends decided to open the door. There was very little to see. They could barely make out grass with a path winding from it, the shadows of trees in the distance. But it was the sky that frightened them into slamming the door shut.

You see, in this city, this city of perpetual light, no one could ever see the stars. The street lights, the spot lights, the lights on the building, the lights from out of the windows, and the large city lights used to evoke a feeling of safety, made it so bright that the stars were never seen. The moon would pass by sometimes, either unnoticed or mistaken for another light.

So when Alistair and Railing opened the door and looked out at the world beyond the city, they saw the stars for the first time. And the apparition terrified them. The darkness blazed with a thousand lights and the young men trembled. It wasn't that the spectacle was frightening in itself, but they had never seen anything so glorious. And when a soul first beholds true glory, it has no choice but to fear.

Although the sight of the stars terrified the men, they could not help but think about them all the next day long. It was the kind of fear that came with a thrill, was as fascinating as it was terrifying.

For Alistair, the memory of the stars made the longing in his heart unbearable. Everything around him seemed even uglier than it had before, weak and vulgar beside the transcendent beauty of the stars. He dreamed more everyday, and as he worked he hated the stamps in his hands, despised the drudgery of his life.

Railing's fear had disappeared almost as soon as he slammed the door shut. Someone such as he, with a soul that was made to live in the outdoors, found a sudden resonance in the lights of the heavenly night. That thing he had longed for, had searched and searched for without even knowing what it was, had been laid bare before him. Immediately, he knew what he wanted, or rather, where he belonged. He wanted to be outside, where he could be under that marvelous sky.

It only took two days for the friends to meet again. Their excitement would not let them wait a moment longer. This time, they opened the door with more giddiness than anticipation.

The stars were out again as before, but this time the moon had risen also. Both men drew in a breath of surprise, instantly falling in love. The moonlight danced in their eyes, filling them with wonder, fanning a fire in their souls. For both the hunter and the poet love the moon. The poet loves the moon for the strange and mysterious light it covers the night with. The hunter loves it because the moon is his mistress, and the lone companion to any who stalk the night.

The two held the door open and stared as long as their daring held. This time, fear of discovery forced them to slam the door shut. They both looked around with boyish and irrepressible smiles, fearful they would be discovered, and left after vowing to return the following night.

At first, both men were satisfied to return to the door every night and gaze out over the night sky. They had finally found what they had been looking for. After the first few visits they began to discern the trees and the dirt path that wound off into the darkness. Each time they met at the door they held it open a little longer, yet neither dared leave the safety of the walls.

As weeks passed by, the men noticed that their longing had actually grown worse. Alistair began snapping at people he worked with. Railing couldn't sleep at night. Both men were filled with a rush of energy neither had felt before. The only remedy they could think of was to look out the door even more than they already were.

Finally, they decided to open the door during the day. What they saw made their amazement soar. It looked a little like the park, but grander, more powerful. The trees towered tall and proud, the path that wound through the forest beckoned them to walk on it. And there was some other quality the forest had that the park did not, something neither Railing or Alistair knew, and if they had been born in a younger age, they would know the feeling as awe. But since there was nothing in their age to fill the people with awe, they had forgotten the word altogether.

One thing they did know is that both men wanted to be in that forest, wanted to know what lay beyond, past what they could see. It took every bit of will to keep themselves from running directly into the woods. Fear as well held them back, for they had never encountered anything so full of danger. Their hearts leapt at the very thought.

What the daylight did more than anything else was give them a measure of courage. Something about the sunlight does that. While at night the men never would have dared to step beyond the wall, in daylight the thought overwhelmed them. It is in the nature of light to make something less frightening than it seems in the dark.

It took three more visits until they finally dared step off the sidewalk onto the dirt path. Railing did it first, not even thinking about it. One moment, he stared at the forest, his feet itching to chase through the trees. The next, he heard Alistair's warning.

"Railing," Alistair whispered. "You stepped out."

Railing looked down at his feet as if to confirm what Alistair said. He shrugged and stepped further, reveling in the feel of the soft earth beneath him.

Alistair looked nervously over his shoulder and followed his friend. The outdoors were not as natural an element to him as Railing, so his steps were smaller and more hesitant. He kept looking over his shoulder to make sure the door still waited.

They looked around, wide-eyed, frightened yet fascinated. The beauty of the woods and the grass drew them on, but the sheer enormity of the forest, just the feel of the latent power within, tempered their fascination with fear. A kind of reverence touched them, sensing something powerful beyond anything else they had ever seen. They wanted to run and at the same time did not want to profane the ground with their play.

The two friends felt the grass, breathed deep of the fresh air and caressed the trunk of the nearby trees. They ventured as far as they dared, which happened to be only a few feet from the safety of the door. But for them it may as well have been a pilgrimage to the strangest and most distant corners of the earth.

Every day they returned and walked further and further. Alistair would always look back to make sure the door stood open, fearful it might disappear. Eventually they worked up to step out of sight of the door, just as the path bent into the forest.

Neither man knew what to make of the forest. Nor did they know what to do with it. They walked up and down the path, not far, but further than any had walked in many generations. Sometimes they laid in the grass and stared up at the sky. Once they even did so at night, and happened to catch a falling star streak across the dark space.

Life inside the city grew more unbearable for both of them. The hours and the days they passed in the city were mere interludes until they could both get outside the walls again. Eventually they forgot to fear that they might get caught. A new life stirred in them, something foreign to the safety of the city. They hated the ugliness and the noise and the grayness of the streets and steel walls more everyday.

One day, the two spent more time than usual out in the forest. They hiked down the path further than they had before. This was only about two hundred yards, but for them they could have been on the moon. Railing caught sight of a preying mantis, and the two watched the creature in wonder. So transfixed were they staring at the weird insect that they lost track of time altogether. When they got back to the city it was almost dark – and the door was closed.

Panic ripped through Alistair as he tugged on the door. It wouldn't budge an inch. Railing tried it too but couldn't get it to move. He pulled his key out and was horrified to see that their side of the door had no lock.

Alistair banged on the door, screaming for help. Railing banged too, though not nearly as hard or desperate. The sun sank down on the other side of the city and darkness fell over them. After a while Railing gave up, and an hour later Alistair did too. Both men huddled against the wall and watched out in terror at the night around them. It didn't seem so beautiful anymore.

Sleep eventually overtook them and they spent a dreamless night, waking with the sun high and the dew just beginning to dry. Alistair turned around and continued to bang on the door. Railing didn't bother. Instead, he stared off down the path that wound deep into the forest.

Hunger overtook the men as the morning wore on. Alistair fell down and wept, writhing under the strange sensation of uncertainty.

"We need to find something to eat," Railing said to Alistair as he cried.

"There is no food here," he said, noticing for the first time that there were no food stalls outside the walls.

Neither man had ever to contend with hunger in their lives. Nor did they know a thing about where food came from. Anytime they were hungry they went to a food stall and bought food. Food was only part of life's background in the city.

"Maybe we can find some," Railing suggested. "I don't think anybody will hear us banging. Besides, even if they do I have the key out here."

Resigned to his fate, Alistair consented and the pair set off down the road. Once he had accepted that they couldn't get back in and had gone a ways through the forest his mood began to lighten. Even through his hunger and fear Alistair felt a twinge in his gut that strangely resembled happiness. Deep within him he knew that this is what he wanted all along. He was setting off on adventure.

Part II

All day long the pair walked, seeing neither man or beast.

The woods continued to stretch out around them, the path winding deeper and deeper into the forest. Their hunger would gnaw at them, then surprisingly drift away. Alistair would grow afraid sometimes, looking around the endless range of trees, then the beauty of the forest would seduce him and he would forget how desperate his situation was and enjoy his walk.

They went to sleep hungry that night, huddled against each other beneath a giant oak. As morning peered through the trees they rose again, both of them parched and trembling with hunger. Destiny left them no choice but to travel on, so they did, plunging deeper into the forest.

Hunger and thirst began to transform the young adventurers. For more than two days they had neither drink or food, and though their bellies ached and their mouths became dry, something deep rose in them. Hardship brought out something that had been hidden by generations of comfort. Though Alistair nor Railing knew or understood what was happening, the heart of true manhood began to beat in them, filling their blood with virtue and courage. The further they walked, the more hungry and thirsty they became, the less they feared and the more they anticipated what lay down the path.

As darkness fell on the third day the two men heard the sounds of water gurgling nearby. They darted off the path toward the sound and discovered water bubbling from a rock and making a stream through the forest. Neither had seen a spring before but both filled up their hands and drank deeply, savoring the clean taste of pristine water. Still hungry, though satisfied, they decided to sleep near the spring that night.

Before either of the two adventurers dozed off a delicious aroma startled them fully awake. The unmistakable smell of cooking food reached them. They bolted up and hurried towards the smell, heedless of any danger, half-expecting a food stall to be waiting for them in the shadow of the trees. Instead, a cottage came into sight, smoke rising out of the chimney and the air thick with a savory aroma.

The men found the door cracked open and a yellow light coming from within. They peered tentatively inside. It was mostly dark, a single room lit only by the fire and a few candles. A beautiful young woman sat by the fire, wrapped in a thick blanket.

At first the men could only stare. Over the fire they saw a cut of meat roasted on a spit. The warmth of the house beckoned them in as well as the smell of cooking food. But they hesitated, warned by a situation they had never encountered and being so new to fear.

Eventually, the woman sensed them and turned.

"There is no reason to stand there cold and hungry," she said with a voice like music. "Why don't you come in and enjoy the fire?"

Without hesitation the two men stumbled in. They stood awkwardly, not knowing how to act. Their eyes alternated between staring at the beautiful woman and looking hungrily at the cooking meat.

"If you tell me your stories I will give you food and shelter for the night," the woman told them, seeing the hunger in their eyes.

The men eagerly agreed and laid out their whole lives in a few, sparse moments. So little had they experienced both men were ashamed at how easily their whole existence could be summed up. Until they had decided to walk through the door along the steel wall, there was precious little to tell about their lives.

The woman, though, was fascinated about life in the city. Up until then she had been cold and distant, only vaguely interested in the men. But upon hearing where they came from she sprang up and smiled at them, suddenly treating them as if they were royalty.

"I am Bella," she told them. "Never have I had such distinguished guests in my home. Please, whatever is mine is yours."

Immediately, Bella began to serve them. She carved meat and filled their plates. She produced a pitcher of beer and filled and refilled their glasses. Both Alistair and Railing ate until they were full, the meat tasting especially delicious to their deprived appetites. With full stomachs and the beer warming their blood they stretched out contentedly by the fire.

When the fire died down to only the glow of embers, Bella rose and took them to their own rooms. She left each man in a soft bed, placed a candle by the bed and promised to have another meal for them in the morning.

Both men had vivid dreams that night. Railing found himself over a valley as broad and wide as the eye could see. He sat atop a horse, and though the situation was strange to him he felt oddly comfortable astride the animal. Other men beside him were also mounted, each of them holding a long spear.

Railing hefted the spear, thrilled at the feel of the weapon in his hand. Below him in the valley a herd of massive elk and deer roamed without worry or concern. In their midst strode one animal that stood out among the others – a white doe, smaller, more delicate, but also pure and lovely to behold.

With a whoop the hunters charged down the valley, each one intent on impaling a kill of their own.

A stampede quickly broke out as the hunters plunged into the herd. A few of the men hurled their spears at smaller elk, but most rode towards the white doe.

The agile deer danced through the shower of spears that fell harmlessly around her. She dodged the attacks with almost a playful exuberance. Railing aimed and threw his own spear, the blade sinking deep into the startled animal's flesh.

As the white deer stumbled Railing felt a rending in his own breast. It felt as if his heart was exploding. He watched the deer struggle and he had the unnerving certainty that he felt exactly the pain of the wounded doe. Pain continued to rip through him with panic. He felt life slip from him when he suddenly awoke, the sun already high in the morning sky.

Alistair dreamt of the beautiful Bella.

Deep in midnight the two danced along a mountaintop, the stars blazing overhead brighter than he ever knew possible. They danced while music played from somewhere that Alistair could not see. He was dizzy with love, hardly able to take his eyes off of the enchanting woman, somehow more beautiful in his dreams than she was in waking life.

The music stopped and Bella's face became gravely serious. She took Alistair's hand and walked him to an old ruin, full of fallen pillars and crumbled walls rising out of the ground. In the midst of the ruins lay a stone altar. Bella stepped out of her clothes, dazzling now as she stood naked in the moonlight. She lay upon the altar and beckoned to Alistair with open arms.

Alistair fell into her embrace and lifted her face to kiss him. Just before their lips touched she stopped him.

"You must pledge your life to me," she whispered. "Pledge your life to me and I will give you pleasure beyond what you could ever imagine."

Alistair opened his mouth to eagerly give that pledge, but no sound came out. He tried to speak but only a hoarse whisper sputtered from his mouth. Bella waited, a frown on her beautiful face as Alistair tried to choke out the words that would not come out.

Alistair grabbed at his throat as his breath stopped up and his lungs burned with sudden urgency. He could neither speak or breathe. Bella still looked at him, turning old before his eyes. Her skin sagged and her hair sprouted grey and wiry. Her luminous and dark eyes yellowed over and sunk into her head.

All Alistair could do was stare in horror as Bella rotted before his very eyes. He tried to reach out to her but dizziness quickly filled his head. A scream stood mute on his lips. Bella shrunk into a dry skeleton. Just before consciousness left him, he awoke.

* * *

Later that morning Alistair and Railing told each other of their strange dreams. They were alone in the cabin. Bella was nowhere to be found but a loaf of hot bread, some butter and cheese, and tea that was still hot waited for them. The two men ate gratefully and talked of what their dreams might mean.

About midmorning the pair was still alone and began to wonder if Bella had been a dream also. With full bellies they could hardly deny she was real.

Eventually, they decided to strike out again and find the road. Alistair was at first hesitant to leave Bella behind, but the awful dream he had of her still evoked fresh fear. As beautiful as she was the horror of the dream was greater yet.

The men left and were not far out when they realized they had no idea where the road was. They had come to the cottage last night from the spring. And while the spring was by the side of the road, they had wandered deep into the woods, seduced by the smell of food. But having never been lost before they were optimistic about finding the road again.

They didn't travel far when a crashing sound came stirring up from behind them. Instinctively the two men turned and stood together as eight horses came bursting through the trees, each bearing a man decked in armor and bearing swords, spears or battle axes.

Alistair and Railing had never seen such weapons. The guards in the city carried only batons, and in emergencies used a gas that made men docile. Though the men didn't know what the weapons were, one look assured them they were deadly things. A sort of dangerous power emanated from them and the men bearing them.

"Intruders in the High Lord's forest!" a man with a plumed helmet cried out as the horses circled the frightened men.

Railing held his baton out defensively. He knew it was a futile gesture. Even if he had been armed as they he could never overcome the odds he faced.

"Throw down your weapons and come quietly," the plumed man demanded. "Perhaps the High Lord will deal mercifully with you."

Railing threw his weapon down immediately and held up his hands.

"This must be a mistake," Alistair spoke up, his voice trembling. "We wandered away from the city and lost our way from the road."

"Crime upon crime!" the plumed man yelled. "Out of their own mouths they confess to two capital crimes! Arrest them!"

Before the men knew what was happening the guards roughly subdued and bound them. Chains clamped down upon their wrists and ankles and they were forced to run behind the horses in stilted, painful steps. Iron shackles bit into their tender skin as they ran, goaded by threats and curses from the guards. The pain was eclipsed by the worst fear they had ever felt in their life. For the first time they knew the cold terror of having their lives threatened.

For what seemed like hours the cruel, forced march continued. As afternoon rose high the party came out of the forest and dipped into rolling fields. They came up a rise and a group of houses came into view that surrounded a castle. Even bound and frightened the two adventurers were awestruck, having never seen a castle before. The soldiers plunged them through the village and the gates, stopping in the castle yard before dismounting.

The two men were hustled away without any explanation. They were forced through a small door in the castle and down a dark, winding stair. At the bottom they were rushed through the dungeons, thrown into a cell and had the heavy, iron door slammed and locked behind them.

Alone in the darkness the men finally had a chance for their predicament to set in. The dank smell of mildew and rot, the feel of the rough rock around them and the impenetrable darkness of the dungeon stirred their fears until both men wept.

"What is going to happen to us?" Alistair cried out, first giving vent to his fear.

"I don't know," Railing mumbled. "I don't even know what we have done wrong."

The two men sat in the dungeon for the better part of a day. They had lost all track of time so they did not know what part of the day it was when the dungeon door squealed open and a group of soldiers came in with a burning torch to drag the pair away again.

The guards pushed Alistair and Railing down the dungeon hallway, up a flight of stairs and into a bare room. Their shackles were unlocked and thrown aside. Both men rubbed their sore wrists and ankles, relieved not to have the metal biting into them. A pitcher of water and a clump of stale bread was set on the floor before them.

Despite the bread's hardness the men choked down the meager meal. The water tasted metallic and smelled dirty but they forced it down also.

"Why do you keep us here?" Alistair asked after they had eaten. "What have we done wrong?"

"His Honor the Judge will see you shortly," was all the guard offered in explanation.

So the two men waited. Some hours passed when the door to the room flew open again and the guards stiffened to attention.

"His Honor Judge Highcloth!" one of the guards cried out as the judge swept in ceremoniously.

Judge Highcloth looked over the two men with an obvious air of presumption. He folded his hands in voluminous, black robes and paced the floor. Occasionally he would look up at the men with his deep set, hawkish eyes, seeming even more avian by the prominent nose that jutted from his face.

"You men have been accused of serious crimes," the Judge finally spoke up. "Your arresting guard claims that you men admitted to having left the city and walked along the Forbidden Road."

"I don't understand what we have done wrong," Alistair protested.

Judge Highcloth cut him off with a raised hand.

"Did you or did you not leave the city and travel along the Forbidden Road?" the Judge asked with stern gravity. "This is very serious."

"We did leave the city and travel along the road. But I assure you we did not know it was forbidden."

"This is a very serious matter!" the Judge cried out, his face turning red. "You broke the law by leaving the city and furthered your crime by walking along a road that is forbidden! Do you know how serious this is?"

Alistair and Railing felt more frightened than before. Mostly they feared because they did not understand their crime. Neither one could see the injury of their offense but it was clear the judge was very worked up over the affair.

"Please, just return us to the city and we won't do it again," Alistair pled as Railing nodded his agreement.

"No, no, we cannot," the judge murmured as he shook his head. "This is all too serious."

"What was your intent in walking along that road?" the judge looked up to ask them. "And why did you leave the city in the first place? Was there not a locked door to keep you from leaving?"

Railing looked away from the judge's gaze. He spied a glance at Alistair who himself was staring at the floor.

"I took the key and we unlocked the door," Railing told him. "But we had no intention of leaving. We only wanted to explore the outside for a little bit."

"Explore?" the judge asked with a brow furrowed in confusion. "Whatever would you explore? Don't you know this is serious?"

"We didn't know. I promise we didn't know how serious this all was."

"Why did you travel the road?" the judge asked. "What was your intent in walking the road?"

"We became locked out of the city," Railing explained. "There was no other option than to follow the path through the forest."

"But this is even more serious," the judge solemnly intoned.

He paced the floor again, shaking his head and muttering to himself about how serious the situation had become.

"Are you sure you had no other intentions in walking down the road?"

"We promise," Railing assured the judge. "We walked down the road only because we had no choice."

"You could have walked through the forest," the judge suggested. "Why didn't you walk through the forest?"

"Well..." Railing began, more than a little confused. It had seemed natural to him to walk down the path. He had to think to figure out why.

"We could have gotten lost in the forest," he finally answered. "Only by walking on the road could we find our way. It's a road, it has to lead somewhere, doesn't it?"

"LEAD SOMEWHERE!" the judge screamed in apparent agitation. "What do you mean to suggest by leading somewhere?! Do you want to go somewhere?! Where do you want to go?!"

"I don't know!" Railing yelled back, surprising even himself. "We were both tired of being in the same place. We wanted to go somewhere."

The judge paced again and scratched his chin. The muttering rose up again. Finally he looked up at the two men as if he had reached a decision.

"I have decided this is all very serious," he informed the pair. "This case must move on to the High Lord. Only he can decide in cases of such momentous gravity. You will remain imprisoned, in this room here, until the High Lord can see you."

With a flourish of his robes the judge turned and stormed out of the room. The guards snapped to attention again and saluted the retreating official.

"His Honor the Judge Highcloth!" one of the guards cried out again.

It was the next day until the men were brought food and

water again. Their new prison, though, was more appealing than the dungeon. Even though the stone walls and floor were cold, and they had no place to sleep or sit except the cold floor, there was a small, barred window high up the wall. Through the iron bars daylight filtered through, letting the men at least get a feel for what time of day it was.

When the prison door finally opened, what must have been the ugliest woman that either Alistair or Railing had ever seen walked in with a tray of bread and water. She was so ugly that the two men stared in horrified fascination, wondering how a human being could have become so hideous.

It wasn't just that the woman was fat. It was the way the fat hung on her. Just below her hips the legs bulged out like little pillows stuffed down her silk dress. And the fact that the dress fit tightly to her body made the fat above her elbows and the pudge that rounded her entire mid-section stand out with distinctive disproportion.

It wasn't her odd features either, the eyes that stood way to far apart, the wide forehead, the drooping mouth of crooked lips that revealed a gaggle of twisted teeth when it smiled. It wasn't the nest of wiry hair or the pale skin splotched with sickly, red circles. It wasn't even the hideous makeup that was caked on the misshapen face like clown's paint.

What made the woman so particularly hideous was the way she moved, the manner in which she carried herself. The way the woman swayed, the deliberate swish of the bulging hips, the batting of the wide eyes and the twisted smile she flashed at them all seemed to be the moves of a seductive woman who used her beauty to charm the hearts of men. But on this woman, this grotesque figure that looked to be patched together by a blind mad scientist, the gestures highlighted her ugliness.

"Hello boys," the woman grated out of a voice that

sounded like rocks tumbling. "I brought you something...tasty."

She laughed and both men jumped in horror. The sound that came out her mouth would have been a scream had it not been for the twisted smile and the hands thrown in the air to show amusement.

"I'm Leanna," the woman tried to breathe out seductively, though it came out like a cough. "I believe you met my sister, Bella."

Alistair coughed and Railing stared in disbelief. Neither of the men could imagine two sisters who looked less alike. For a moment neither could believe what she said was true.

"You look nothing alike," Alistair let out before he could stop himself.

"Oh stop it," Leanna said as she swatted at him and flashed her eyes as if Alistair had just paid her a compliment.

"You boys are bad, I'm going to have to keep an eye on you."

She barked her awful laugh again and turned to walk away. The men could only stare in horror as she swayed her hips in wild exaggeration.

Leanna returned everyday. Everyday she brought with her dried bread and the coppery water. Everyday she flirted with the men and flashed her hideously grotesque eyes. One day she even tried to feed Alistair at which the young man threw his arms up and backed away in wide eyed terror. Confused, the ugly woman threw the crumb of bread down and stalked out of the room.

The day after that Bella came with their bread and water.

After almost a week of being tortured by Leanna's horrid face, seeing Bella was like the first fall of rain on a desert. Alistair sighed and Railing smiled contentedly.

"Bella, oh it's good to see you again," Alistair said in relief.

"Why do you say that?" Bella shot out, her face furrowed

in suspicion.

"Who wouldn't want to see a face as beautiful as yours," Alistair told her.

Bella slammed the tray of food on the floor and stormed from the room.

The next day Bella returned and set the food down without a word. She turned and walked stiffly to the door. Just as she placed her hand on the handle she turned again.

"I know you must be angry that I turned you in to the High Lord," she said as she looked at Alistair. "But there is no reason for you to be cruel to me, a pitiful woman."

"What cruelty have I done to you," Alistair said as he raced over to her side. "I have only called you beautiful, is that cruel?"

"You mock me because I am ugly," Bella retorted, tears filling her eyes.

"How can anyone call you ugly?" Alistair argued, astounded anyone could think otherwise. "You are one of the most radiant creatures I have ever encountered."

"The High Lord told me you would do this," Bella spat.

"Do what?"

"Make fun of my ugliness by calling me beautiful. Everyone knows how ugly I am. Everyone knows I could never be as beautiful as my sister."

Alistair could not help but laugh. Mistaking his humor, Bella turned and stalked to the door. Alistair grabbed and spun her around.

"I only laugh because I would never compare you to that hideous thing you call a sister. You are beauty itself. She doesn't even deserve to stand in your shadow."

Bella looked as if she repressed a smile. She wanted to be pleased but could not allow herself to feel so.

"Ridiculous," she said and spun around and left.

Something changed in Alistair at that moment. Later that night, as the moonlight filtered in through the sole window of the room, he stretched out on the cold, stone floor and dreamed of Bella. Many times in his life he had been infatuated, been seduced, laid in the embrace of many a gorgeous young lady. But never had he felt like this. Had it not been for the pesky confines of his body he could have soared. It happened as he argued with Bella, saw that flash of fire in her eyes and he felt a fire light in him. For the first time in his life, Alistair was in love.

From then on Bella brought the meager food to Alistair and Railing. She flashed looks at Alistair who stared back intently, drinking in her every gaze. She would smile at Railing and talk to him, making an effort to ignore Alistair.

Over the next few days they talked freely, telling Bella everything once again about the city, why they left and why they set out on the road. Railing did most of the talking, as Bella continued to ignore Alistair, only stealing glances at him from time to time, looking angry when she did.

Alistair grew despondent. Thinking the attention Bella lavished on Railing was a sign of her love for him, he felt despair rise in the pit of his stomach. Every night he stared at the lone window, dreaming of Bella's face rising over him. He did not harbor resentment towards Railing, who for his part seemed not to notice any of these things. For sure he thought the woman beautiful, and enjoyed her attention. But for Railing, if he were to have a wide open field present itself he would have no hesitation in leaving Bella behind to chase through the endless hunt.

Another week passed when the guards returned, roughly picking the pair up and hustling them out the door. They were pushed through the castle, down halls hanging with weapons and armor, by tapestries and wall sconces. Finally, they were led into a chamber that was long, pillared and full of people. At the end stood a dais topped with a throne.

At first they could make out little of the figure on the throne. The guards forced them through the hall. They noticed courtiers staring openly at them, whispering behind their hands. All of the women in the court were as ugly as Leanna, thickly painted, fat and misshapen of face. The men looked dainty and pale, waving perfumed handkerchiefs in front of powdered faces.

The men were brought before the dais and thrown down on the marble floor. The courtiers gathered around as Alistair looked up at the seated figure on the throne.

Opposed to the effeminate men and the ugly women of the court, the High Lord sat beautiful and strong upon his throne. Muscular arms gripped the arms of his royal chair. Swarthy and flawless skin covered handsome features. Dark hair flowed down to broad shoulders. Clear blue eyes regarded the prisoners with a hint of amusement in them. Within them Alistair could see neither cruelty or kindness.

"The High Lord Rabon holds court to consider the fate of these two prisoners from the city!" a herald cried out, his voice booming through the pillared court. "Both men are charged with the high crimes of leaving the city confines and traveling along the Forbidden Road!"

The High Lord Rabon looked down at the men with a smile.

"How do you answer these charges?" Rabon asked them.

"We can only plead ignorance, lord," Alistair answered. "We did not know that either action was forbidden."

"Did the city not have a locked door at the wall?" Rabon asked.

"It did."

"And was there not a guard there to prevent any from trying to leave the city?"

"Yes, lord," Alistair answered, casting his eyes down.

"And yet you claim that you did not know it was forbidden to leave the city?" Rabon dug his inquiry.

"My lord, the fault is mine," Railing spoke up. "I was the guard that was supposed to keep people from trying the door. I took the key and used it to open the door. I knew it was forbidden but did not know why."

The High Lord regarded the two men for a moment in silence. His gaze shifted from one to the other. Alistair imagined he saw a flash of hatred cross the High Lord's face.

"How long have you been a guard?" Rabon finally asked.

"For ten years."

"And how often in those ten years have you tried to leave the city?"

"Only the one time, my lord."

"And how many people have tried to leave the city in those ten years?"

"Only myself and Alistair."

Rabon stroked his short beard and eyed Alistair suspiciously. Alistair trembled inside, knowing where the High Lord was leading with his questions.

"When did it finally occur to you to open the door you knew to be forbidden?" Rabon continued.

"It was after I met Alistair," Railing answered, his head down.

"Whose idea was it to open the door?"

Railing didn't answer. He stole a glance at his friend who was also staring at the floor. He looked around, desperate for something to say other than the truth.

"Answer the High Lord!" the herald boomed out so loud that both men jerked in surprise.

"Both of us thought to open the door," Railing mumbled.

Rabon held up a hand to cut off any further talk. He regarded the men for another silent moment, stroking his thin beard, before speaking.

"Do you know this woman?" the High Lord asked Alistair, indicating Leanna who leaned on the throne. The ugly woman glared down at him through hideously long eye lashes.

"I do, my lord," Alistair answered.

"Do you find her beautiful?" Rabon asked.

"She is not to my taste," Alistair answered, not wanting to be cruel.

"But do you find her beautiful, pleasing to look at?"

"Others might, but I do not."

A murmur, almost scandalous, rippled through the courtiers. Some laughed and shook their heads, others stared at Alistair as if he were mad.

"And this woman here," Rabon asked having a guard push Bella up to stand before him. "Do you find her beautiful?"

"I do, my lord," Alistair answered. "I find her very beautiful."

The room erupted in laughter. Bella hung her head down, unable to face the mocking laughter.

"Are you sure you find such a grotesque woman attractive?" Rabon pressed. "After all, every one here can see that she is by far the ugliest woman around here."

Alistair looked up at Bella and his heart swelled. Standing meek among the painted and bloated courtiers, smooth-skinned, dark and luminous eyes, pristine and lovely, Bella glowed. The stirrings of the poet moved his mind and words that had no origin in his brain flowed out of him.

"She is as radiant as the sun and as lovely as the moon. If she were placed among the stars of heaven, her beauty would outshine them all. Of all the women I have beheld, there is none that is her equal."

For a moment the room was stunned into silence. It had been past any man's memory that words of even such a simple eloquence had been uttered at that court. Even Bella dared to look up, her eyes fixing upon Alistair. Tears pooled in her eyes and a smile crept up to her lips before she dropped her head again.

Rabon let out a hard, barking laugh. Alistair could tell it

was forced. The court eventually followed the High Lord's lead, straining to make their laughter sound genuine. When the High Lord looked down at Alistair again he wore the traces of anger and fear across his face.

"I have decided what my judgement shall be," the High Lord intoned ominously. "It is clear that this Alistair here is an irredeemable liar and deceiver. Who else would tell such blatant untruths as to say this hideous woman here is beautiful? All the while he claims her much more beautiful sister, Leanna, is ugly. Everyone can see the opposite is true. This proves that Alistair is a liar and deceiver.

"On the other hand, his friend Railing had faithfully stood his post as a guard for ten years without questioning his orders or daring to go out of the city. It wasn't until Alistair arrived and stirred his heart with temptation that he was deceived and decided to leave the city with this scoundrel. The fault for the crime clearly lies with him.

"My judgement is this. Alistair from the city will be sentenced to hard labor in the mines until his lying is reformed. When he finally looses his deceitful ways and tells the truth he will be free to rejoin life as a peasant laborer. Until then he will be chained to rock and forced to lie in darkness. It shall be as I have spoken.

"Take him away!"

Before he could utter a word of protest Alistair was pulled roughly from the assembly and out of the castle. In the courtyard a prison cart waited. The guards hurled him inside and locked the door.

As the cart rolled away Alistair peered out of the barred window, looking back at the castle with a growing fear. Into the mines he was being sent. A fate that sounded worse than the city he escaped.

All past him the countryside rolled by. Even despite himself Alistair could not help but love the gently rolling hills and the lanes of pasture and crops growing in the distant fields. He appreciated them even more knowing he would not see them again for a long time.

The wagon rolled through the hills and up a crag of mountain. The wooden wheels creaked on the high, twisting road. They rose up until they were no more trees except empty skeletons bare of leaves and black rock blasted by a cold wind.

Alistair was pulled out of the cart when they reached the top. A pair of guards ushered him through the mouth of a cave and down through the twisting depths of the mountains. All around him Alistair could see thin and bedraggled figures chained to the rock, pick in hand, digging into the mountain.

Down past all the other workers they pushed Alistair. A chain was strapped to his leg, the other end connected to a ring pounded into the rock. The guards left Alistair alone in the darkness.

Just when Alistair began to believe he would be left there alone forever he saw a light coming towards him. A thin and bedraggled figure limped down the shaft, bearing a torch and a tall basket.

"Greetings master," the man coughed and set the basket down.

He pulled a pick from the basket and a candle. He lit the candle and handed the pick to Alistair.

"We dig everyday when the candle is lit," the man explained. "You've got 'til the candle burns out to fill the basket with broken rocks. If the foreman comes by and sees the basket full you get your meal. If the basket ain't full you get nothin. If you find a chunk of silver, you don't have to fill the basket. You get double portions and you can rest the remainder of the day. Got it? Now get to work."

Still reeling from the events of the day Alistair reluctantly lifted his pick and began digging at the earth. When the candle had burned down his body ached all over and the basket was hardly half full with broken rocks. The foreman came by and grunted at the basket and had a helper lift it away.

"Maybe tomorrow you'll earn a meal," he said, turning to leave.

"Where am I to sleep tonight?" Alistair asked the retreating foreman.

"Right where you are," he answered as he left, taking the meager light with him.

Never in his life had Alistair felt so lonely. He lay in total darkness, chained to a rock and sleeping on the stone floor in the bowels of a cave. He had never known such total oblivion. He wanted to cry but somehow his tears would not come. His body ached too much for anything but sleep.

Before he knew it a torch flared up in his face and the man who had brought him his pick and basket hovered over his face.

"Rise up you worthless sod," he laughed through broken teeth. "Time to work at it again."

Hungry and sore Alistair roused himself up and set to his pick, determined to fill the basket up. The meager candle light shone like the sun in the dark mine, and after a time Alistair fell into a rhythm of labor. Just before the candle burned down he had the basket full of broken rocks.

The foreman grunted at the basket again, his approval sounding a lot like his disappointment. A helper heaved the basket onto his back and carried it away.

"Congratulations, you'll get supper tonight," the foreman said.

That promised supper consisted of a heel of bread, weak broth and a cup of water. Alistair gobbled it all down gratefully. No sooner had he eaten than sleep took him over, full of dreams of rock and weak candle light.

For many days life went on like this for Alistair. And

though he managed to fill the basket, he grew weaker and weaker because the work was harder than the poor nutrients he received. He found himself daydreaming during his work, but to his surprise he dreamt of the city. As he hammered at rock he imagined and remembered walking down streets filled with food and sleeping in a soft bed. He even thought fondly of his job at the factory, punching cards over and over again. Anything, he thought, was better than the awful mine. He cursed the dreams that had brought him to that terrible place and worked harder and harder everyday to fill his basket.

One day, as he had just finished his meal a torch came down the tunnel towards him. He blinked back the bright light and peered up at Bella who stood over him, radiant as ever in the cruel and bare mine. All at once every ounce of regret left him. Anything, he thought to himself, was worth seeing this vision, if even for a moment.

"Bella," he breathed, amazement rich in his voice.

The woman didn't answer, but only stared down at Alistair coldly, her expression unreadable. Despite her coldness towards him he could not help loving her.

"Was it true what you said earlier?" she asked, sounding angry. "Do you really find me beautiful?"

"Every beauty in the world must hang her head in shame in your presence," he swore, meaning every word he said. "I have seen no woman who is your equal."

Immediately Bella broke into tears and threw herself at Alistair's feet. She moaned something he could not understand, muffled by sobs. As much as Alistair tried to comfort her she would not be consoled. Several minutes passed before she could rise and speak.

"Why do you say such things to me?" she asked him tearfully. "It tears me in two to hear them?"

"Why would any woman not want to hear how beautiful she is?" Alistair asked, truly perplexed by Bella's behavior.

"Ever since Rabon took over I have lived in the shadow of my sister, and always told that she was beautiful while I was horribly ugly. I would never marry or be loved I am so hideous."

Alistair was stunned into silent disbelief, wondering how such an incredible situation could ever have come about. He asked Bella this very thing.

The woman then set out her miserable story from beginning to end. Her mother had died after giving birth to her. Growing up it was only her, her older sister Leanna, and their father, a young nobleman named Cedric. From the first Leanna always demanded to have treasures and toys, baubles of gold, trinkets of jewelry. Out of guilt her father relented, feeling sorry that their mother had died.

Bella, on the other hand, loved her father deeply and wanted nothing but to be near him. Leanna was naturally jealous, and the more she resented Bella the more her appearance changed. Other than this they lived happily together in the keep.

One day a rumor reached them that a lord named Rabon was calling himself the High Lord and claimed to have rule over the whole land. Bella was but a little girl when all these things happened. Still she remembered her father being one of the few that resisted Rabon, how after a crushing defeat he barely made it home with the High Lord's forces close on his heels. Tired and wounded he spoke to her, told her to always stay true and wait for the King to come that had been promised from old.

Cedric was taken to prison and the girls carted off to Rabon's court. Leanna was immediately hailed a beauty of the land and took a place of honor with the High Lord. Bella, on the other hand, was told she was too horribly ugly to be anything but a laughingstock for the nobles. She was derided and mocked at court, made to feel ugly and worthless, and when she was old enough, given a cottage in the woods appropriate for the hideous troll that she was.

"But they are liars," Alistair promised her. "It is you who are the beautiful one. All those women at court are ogres, disgusting and painted like dressed up pigs."

Bella wept again and covered her face.

"My father used to always tell me the same thing," she remembered in tears. "He would tell me what a beautiful girl I was. It has been so long since I have heard it I could hardly believe it was true. But it only makes my misery complete. I do not deserve your love."

"Why would you say such a thing?"

"I have betrayed you," Bella said, turning her head away from Alistair's stare.

Alistair reached out and turned her head so that she faced him. He gently stroked her cheek and wiped the tear away that flowed down her face.

"Tell me what you have done," he said. "I could never be angry with you."

She looked up at him as if struggling to believe what he said, then nodded her head reluctantly.

"Rabon has always been looking out for anyone who has left the city, and been especially vigilante to catch anyone who dares walk along the Forbidden Road. When you came into my cottage I turned you in so that I might have a scrap of honor from Rabon's table. Both you and your friend had broken two of our most sacred laws. I knew he would be pleased. Then he asked me to spy on you when he saw you immune to Leanna's beauty, to find out what I could of you. Even now I come on Rabon's orders, to see if you have yet been broken."

"Why are we not allowed to leave the city?" Alistair asked. "That is the way our life has always been," she answered. "We have always lived separately and we have always feared what lies within the city. Rabon especially hates the city. He says it is full of men who hate us and wish to destroy our lives."

"But what about the road? Why are we forbidden to walk the road?" Alistair asked.

Bella looked back into the darkness, checking to see if anyone was close by. Only the darkness surrounded them. Still, she leaned in close and whispered to him.

"It has been rumored that at the end of the road is a weapon that will destroy Lord Rabon," Bella said quietly. "For until now nothing has been able to hurt him. It may even be he is powerless along the road itself. But whatever it is the road haunts his nightmares and he promises a great reward to anyone who helps him capture those who would dare walk it."

"So that is why he treats me so harshly," Alistair surmised. "But what has he given you as reward?"

"I only ask for my father's body," she said, dropping her head down to weep anew. "He died after five years in prison and was tossed into the valley of the dead. I only want his bones returned so that I may bury them properly. Rabon keeps giving me this promise but he never delivers on it."

Alistair nodded his head and retreated into silent thought. A restless energy took over him, a desire to help Bella, to win her heart thoroughly. But the bite in his ankle reminded him of his captivity, his helplessness. His mind turned over and over, trying vainly to think how he could help.

"But I cannot cause you any more harm," Bella told him. "My father would be disappointed that I have not remained true. Here, I have brought you this."

Bella produced a hooded lantern and a wrapped cloth. She pulled the shutter up and the lamp brought forth a brilliant light.

"This lamp is magic," she told him. "My father gave it to me before he was captured. The flame never dies. Not once have I put oil in it and it has never gone out. I have hidden it from Rabon all these years. Here, you put the shade down and no one will see the light. Lift it back up and you will have all the light you need."

"I cannot take this treasure from you," Alistair tried to refuse. "It is the last gift from your father."

"You must take it," she insisted. "My father would want me to help you. You can keep the light shining after your candle has burned out. When the guards look down the cavern they will think it is the candle that burns. When you have filled your barrel then close the shade and hide the lantern. That way you will have food every night."

"Thank you," Alistair said, gratefully taking the lantern. "But even with this my days are numbered. The food we get is hardly enough to live by. I will only waste away slower."

"Then take this too," she pressed the cloth bundle into his hands. "This is sweet tack. Sailors take with them on long voyages because it keeps well and is full of sugar. It will give you energy but eat it sparingly. Maybe fortune will change and provide you with a better opportunity soon."

Alistair nodded and took the gifts, grateful for what she had done. Bella looked down the shaft, seeing a pair of lights coming towards them.

"My time is up," she said. "Do not let them find the gifts, and do not lose hope. Come to me one day."

She leaned in and brushed her lips over his. They were softer and more divine than in his dreams. A dizziness came over him that made him want to laugh. She smiled down at him, her face alight with warmth, then turned and hurried away.

* * *

Over the coming days Alistair attacked his work with new vigilance. When his candle came close to sputtering out he would open the shade of the lantern. The guards, looking down the corridor, only saw light, and believed it was his candle. When he had filled his basket Alistair would pull shut the shutter of the lantern and hide it in a crevice in the rock. The foreman would come by, see the basket full, and Alistair would receive his meager rations. Alone in the dark he would find the hard biscuits Bella had given him. He might dare a small sliver of light from the lantern and eat a bite of the bread. The sweet but hard biscuit seemed to fill him up, no matter how small his meal was.

Over the next days Alistair regained some of his strength. And with the return of his strength came the return of hope. Although he knew as long as he remained in the mines his situation would not change, he also began to believe that he could liberate himself.

He did not know how deep the mine stretched into the earth. And before he did not think he could risk it in the dark. But with Bella's lantern he could plumb the depths of the cave, and with her biscuits he might last a few days, perhaps finding a way out.

No sooner had he resolved to do this than he began working on the chain that bound him. The very next morning, as soon as the foreman brought him his work candle and left, Alistair pounded on his chain with the pick. He was surprised at how easily the chain split. He quickly grabbed up his bundle of bread and the lantern and set off down the cavern.

Deep he traveled into the bowels of the earth. Down through twisting caverns, into the heart of the mountain, Alistair hurried through the caves, fearful a pursuit of guards might be on his heels. What seemed like hours he went deeper and deeper.

When exhaustion finally came over him Alistair laid down on the rocks to catch his breath. He ate a bit of the bread Bella had brought him and closed his eyes. The lamp still burned when he opened them again. He had no idea what time it was and no way to tell. He couldn't remember when last he had looked upon daylight.

Alistair continued on like this. It is impossible to say how much time passed without the light to tell him when one day began and another ended. In his mind Alistair thought months had passed, but surely no more than a day or two had been the actual progress of time. Everything seems longer when you are wandering in the dark with only a lamp to guide you. Despair sets in so easily in your heart, a nagging doubt that you will die buried deep in the bowels of the earth, where no man will ever look upon your awful figure again.

Alistair even began to think that madness crept in upon him. He thought he heard sounds of scurrying in the distance, just beyond the light. Sometimes he thought the sound came from behind him. He would whip around and see nothing but stalactites hanging down like cruel teeth, casting a sinister shadow against the rock wall.

Every once in a while he even thought he glimpsed a figure, just on the edge of light. He would glance a pale, white limb; a foot hastily retreating or a small hand drawing away from the cave wall. Alistair would hurry after the figure any time he thought he saw one, but found only darkness upon darkness.

Once, as he sat to rest, he thought he heard voices echoing through the tunnels. He looked up and strained his eyes in the dark but could see nothing. He looked down and kicked absently at a rock, and again he heard a whisper, just barely.

"The liiight," he thought he heard.

Alistair looked up but could see nothing beyond the circle of light from his lamp.

"Put ouuut the liiight," a whisper rose up.

Alistair grabbed his lamp and stood up. The sounds of scurrying feet pattered through the tunnel. Carefully Alistair set down the lamp and walked away from it.

"Put out the liiight," the voice rose up again.

"The liiight"

"It is soooo briiight."

"Put out the liiiight."

"The liiiight."

"We will feed you."

"We will take you home."

"We will freeee you."

"Put out the liiiiight."

"The liiight."

Carefully Alistair backed up to his lamp and drew the cover. Darkness fell over him and the sounds of motion immediately rose up. Fear trickled over Alistair and he grabbed the lamp up and clutched it to himself, certain it was his only protection.

As his eyes began to adjust to the dark Alistair thought he could make out shapes scurrying through the caves. At first they looked like pale, blue blobs, moving about the tunnel. As the meager light began to filter into his eyes he noticed that the light actually came out of the shapes.

Barely luminescent figures danced nearer to him, hesitant to approach. As they came closer Alistair saw they were small, thin, human-like figures, but like no human he had ever seen. They looked like children, but their skin glowed with a pale, blue light, and he even thought he could see through their skin, and almost made out veins and organs pulsing beneath a translucent dermis.

The only thing that was not blue and glowing were large, circles that must have been eyes. Each was as big as a fist and looked like black holes in the face, but Alistair could have been mistaken for the light was so meager. At best they had to have been large black spots, wide to accommodate the only light that came from their own bodies.

"Come with ussss," one of the figures pulled on his leg

and darted away.

"Come with usss."
"You are so warrrrm."
"You must be fed."
"You are so warrrm."
"We can see how warrrm."
"Come."
"Come with usssss."
"You will love her."
"She is beautiful."
"Pale and beautiful."
"But she is colllld."
"You will warrrrm her."
"You are so warrrm."
"She will love you tooooo."

The creatures would dart up to Alistair and tug on his shirt or pant leg and then scurry away, half-upright and then bending down on all fours.

"Who are you?" Alistair, his voice sounding like a shout compared to the creatures' soft whispers.

A howl rose up from the creatures and they scurried back. Some hissed at him.

"He is tooo loud," some whispered.
"He is tooo warrrm."
"He screeeeams."
"His liiiight burrrrns."
"Commmme."
"Come with usssss."
"Do not screeeeam."

They began to scurry up to Alistair again and pull on his hems. There seemed to be an urgency as well as insistence, as if they wanted his help.

"What do you want?" Alistair whispered to them.
"You musst help herrrr," they whispered back.
"She is sooo cold."

"You will warrrm her."
"You are warrrrm."
"Help who?" Alistair asked.
"The beauuutiful lady."
"She is soooo pretty."
"But she is cold."
"She will looove you."
"You will looove her."
"She is colllld."
"She is sooo pretty."
"Who are you?" Alistair asked the figures scurrying now with greater insistence.
"We are her children."
"But we cannot warrrm her."
"We will feeeed you."
"Commmme."
"You must warrrrm her her."
"You are sooo warrrrm."
"Commmmme."
"You must help herrrr."

A part of Alistair was wary, they were such strange creatures. But another part could see they not only looked like children, they acted like children. Despite their alien appearance, their almost hideousness, they still possessed that childlikeness that is nearly universal. Any adult with compassion is vulnerable to such a plea. That, and the utter loneliness that consumed Alistair compelled him to follow.

Clutching his lantern closer Alistair stepped forward to follow the bluish figures. They scurried off excitedly, almost dancing as they crept on all fours, then leapt on two feet. Alistair half-smiled to himself.

"He commmmes."
"He commmmes to the beauutiful laaaady."
"He is so warrrm."
"We will feeeed him."

"You will be fedddd."

Alistair had no trouble following the figures. The pale, blue light that glowed from their skin grew brighter as his eyes adjusted to the darkness of the cave depths. He did trip over outcropping and rocks, and once slammed his shine into a small stalagmite. He cursed and pulled back the cover on the lamp so only a sliver of light came out to show him what he banged into. Such a howl rose up from the blue children that he quickly replaced the cover and dared not open it again.

They began to take turns and forks in the cave trail. Alistair had well lost his way, but in truth had lost his bearings long ago. His worry faded as the children became more excited.

Eventually the narrow tunnel widened and more children joined in the happy march. They nimbly jumped and bounced through the widening tunnel. All whispering excitedly.

"He commmes."

"He commmmes to warm the laaaady."

"The beautiful laaaady."

"But she is collld."

"We will feeed him."

"He will lovvve her."

"He is sooo warrrrm."

"Sooo warrrrm."

The tunnel widened until it opened into a giant cavern. He couldn't tell the exact dimensions but he heard water dripping in the distance and the echo suggested it was quite large. The cavern swarmed with the glowing blue figures. They danced happily around and whispered so quickly that he could not make out any particular words so that it sounded like a hiss all around him.

The little hands began to push him impatiently. He tried to elbow them away but so many prodded at him that it was pointless. Insistently they led him to a rise in the middle of the cavern, what seemed like a large, stone outcropping that dominated the center of the cavern.

"Goooo."

"Go to herrr."

"She lovvvve yoooou."

"You are so warrrrm."

"We will feed you."

"Feeeed you."

Just as he was pushed to the center of the stone rise the whispers abruptly fell silent. The glowing, blue figures scurried away and left Alistair alone on the flat top of stone.

At first he could see nothing. Then a swaying human figure approached. There was just enough light from the children to see her. And it was decidedly female.

As she came closer Alistair's heart raced. He could make out features as she approached. Her skin, white as snow, her long hair black and her lips crimson and delicious, swam before his hungry eyes. She wore no clothes and seemed unashamed to be naked before him.

Alistair could not keep his eyes off of the voluptuous figure that swayed towards him. She stopped a few inches from him, arms outstretched.

"I feel your warmth," she purred in a voice that sent a trickle of excitement down Alistair's spine. "Come to me, my love. Come and share my love."

A flurry of excited whispers stirred the glowing figures.

"She is pleeeased."

"He is sooo warrrm."

"We will feed him."

"We will feed him to the laaaady."

"The beautiful laaaady will feed on blood."

A hiss came from the woman as Alistair made out the whispers around him. A rustling sounded and two dark shapes rose on either side of her. Alistair hardly saw these, fixated on what looked like two fangs protruding from the woman's blood-red mouth.

Alistair recoiled, backing away from the suddenly frightening figure. Part of him still stared at her, transfixed by her terrible beauty. A hundred hands pushed him back towards the woman, whispering excitedly.

"You must feeed her."

"Feeeed her."

"You are soooo warrrm."

"You must feeed herrr."

Alistair could not fight the tide of hands that pushed him towards certain death. Alistair thrashed around pushing away from the glowing, blue figures. He swatted and backhanded and punched wildly. For every figure he knocked away another crammed in to push him towards the lady.

"You must feeed her."

"You are sooo warrrm."

"Sooo warrrm."

Alistair hunched down to resist. His arms wrapped tightly around the lamp, and suddenly his mind returned to him.

Ripping his arms free Alistair tore the cover off of the lamp and raised it up high. A howl of rage and pain rose up all around him. A shriek, piercing and high, tore from the lady's mouth.

In the light Alistair could fully see the lady's dark beauty. Her pale, naked figure, the flawless, carved shape to her body. But her eyes were black as the pit of night, and the fangs that grew from her mouth distorted the face, and finally he glimpsed the dark figures beside her; a pair of scaled wings that rose from her back.

The lady threw up her hands and the dark wings closed around her like a leathery shell. The children howled and scurried away.

"The liiiight."
"The liiiight."
"Put out the liiiight."

Alistair dared only a glance at the lady closed up in her wings before running down the raised stone. Crowds of the children bolted out of the arc of light that shined from the lamp. He thanked Bella again, pledging his love to her all the more, and ran blindly down the nearest tunnel.

* * *

Alistair had no idea if he was running back into his former captors or away from them, he only ran. He ran through twisting tunnels, up and down rises. It wasn't until his legs ached and his lungs burned for air that he finally slowed down to rest.

Stilling himself as quietly as he could Alistair listened for the sounds of pursuit. He could hear nothing of the strange, pale men. Neither could he see the glow of their blue skin as he swung the lamp around.

Alistair sat down to gather his breath. He rested with his head down, his body trembling with exhaustion and fear. At every sound his nerves jumped and he pulled the light up, looking for any sign of his pursuers.

A streak of color caught his eye as he shone the lamp around him, a burst of red that interrupted the gray and brown rock of the cave. He crept closer and held his light up to inspect it. More color jumped out as he came nearer. It was a painting on the cave wall.

For a moment Alistair forgot his pursuers as he looked over the painted figures, wondering what could have compelled someone to paint this deep in the earth. He marveled at the human figures drawn on the wall, some strange history painted on the rock.

The first picture seemed to be the figures gathering beneath a blue star that streaked past them in the sky. The stick figures held their hands up as the comet passed overhead, as if they were reaching out towards it.

In the next picture the star was on the ground and the figures gathered around it. Blue light streaked from the fallen star and touched the people. Further over were figures of tall men painted blue with streaks of light coming from them.

A chill ran over Alistair as he focused his light on the final pictures. The blue men rose taller, the streaks of light from them longer and a deeper blue. Around them were figures laying down, red paint flowing from their bodies. Even smaller figures, children perhaps, were lifted to their mouths as if the blue giants were about to consume them.

Something about the crude drawings made it feel even more sinister. Perhaps it was the darkness of the cave as well, and Alistair being alone with what seemed like art of the saddest and most desperate kind. He imagined these men coming down into the cave to draw because this was the only place that was safe from whatever monstrosities they painted. Here, deep in the earth, they catalogued the misery and sadness that they could not show above ground. Alistair even imagined the artists knew himself to be the last one to tell what had happened, and even if it were to be in darkness, the story would be told.

With a shiver Alistair hurried on, his exhaustion suddenly gone. He continued on until the tunnel closed in and became smaller and smaller. Frightened the tunnel would end Alistair found himself squeezing through little more than a crack in the cave wall. He sidled through this until it finally opened up into the expanse of a vast underground chamber.

Alistair lifted up the lamp and saw that he stood on the shore of an underground lake. He could not see the top of the chamber he was in nor could he see the far shore. He looked down the passage behind him, hoping he had outrun his pursuers. The passage was dark and the still lake stood like a sheet of glass, not even a ripple on its surface.

Placing the lamp on the cave floor Alistair sat down to catch his breath and leaned back against the cold stone. He didn't notice sleep as it crept up on him. One moment he stared out over the still water, then suddenly the winged lady shot up out of the water. She bared her fangs and hissed, dropping right towards Alistair. Alistair screamed and bolted awake.

Panic washed over him. He breathed a sigh of relief and looked frantically around. No signs of the children creeping nearby.

Strangely, though, he noticed ripples across the surface of the still water. Alistair's imagination ran wild, concocting all sorts of strange creatures that swam beneath the water. His more reasonable side assured him the ripples were only caused by water dripping off of the stalactites.

At any rate, Alistair realized he had to keep moving. He took another bite one of Bella's biscuits, and feeling immediately refreshed, took up the lamp to scan the shore. Following the water down to his right he found the small shore grew smaller and smaller until it disappeared altogether between the water and rock wall.

Just as he turned to go the other way the sound of a splash jerked him around sharply. He lifted the lamp to see the water undulating in deep ripples. Just a rock falling, he told himself, but still hurried on to follow the shore line the other way.

When Alistair reached the opening that had brought him to the lake, he heard the splash again, this time closer. He hurried along faster. The thought came into his head that it was his light that attracted whatever stirred beneath the surface, but he dared not put it out.

Again, the splash came, just outside the border of light. Desperate, Alistair broke into a run along the shore. Like the other side, this thin strip of rock grew more narrow as he ran.

The splash came again so close that drops of water struck his face. Alistair moaned as the shore continued to dwindle.

The surface of the water churned. Out of the corner of his eye he could see the lake frothing. The water boiled and raged, filling the chamber with a roar of distress. The shore still dwindled, growing steadily thinner.

Something dark began to rise out of the water. Alistair ran even as he knew he would surely not survive. Miraculously, when the shore ended he found a staircase cut into the side of the rock.

Without hesitation Alistair leapt onto the staircase and ran as it wound around the outside of the cavern. Beneath him he heard a roar, unmistakably of disappointment and frustration. The whole chamber shook with the sound as the rumble bounced off of the cave walls. Deep within him Alistair felt the vibration, and even the lamp sputtered, but its light remained.

Heedlessly Alistair flew up the narrow, curved stairs. Up and up they carried him. Exhaustion caught up with him and he finally slowed down. The steps showed no signs of ending, so Alistair plodded onward.

Alistair's heart lifted as he noticed the circle growing tighter, as if he were nearing the top of the chamber. Finally, the stairs ended in another tunnel. Alistair stepped off the landing and into the tunnel, and caught his breath. Up ahead was a faint light.

Almost shouting with joy Alistair found his strength again and ran out of the tunnel. He burst out of the cave, finally free from the bowels of the earth, and into a wooded hill. In the valley below he saw the first signs of the sun rising over the horizon. The light was dim, but to his eyes that had not seen sunlight in weeks, it blazed with the power of a thousand suns.

Overcome with joy Alistair spread his hands out and laughed. He stared at the sliver of sun until his eyes teared and he had to look away. Still he laughed. Uncontrollably he laughed. He found he couldn't stop, but he didn't care.

A sudden urge came over him to dance as he laughed. So he danced. It was no dance a person could recognize. He more bounced around than what we could call dancing. But his dance was pure. For the heart of all dance should be joy. And what Alistair felt was pure, uninhibited joy. The dance had no form or dignity, it had no control and was in no way pleasing to the eye, but it was the dance of the universe. Were we not so obsessed with things looking just right or seeming proper, we would notice that the stars dance in the same way.

Eventually his energy waned and Alistair's strange dance came to an end. His laugh faded too but the smile stayed glued to his face. Quicker than he thought possible his eyes were adjusting to the growing light, and he stared at the rising sun, certain he had never seen anything more perfect and welcome in his whole life.

"Sounds like Asher went hungry this time," a voice nearby said.

Alistair whipped around to face one of the strangest looking men he had ever seen. To our eyes he would not have been strange, only old. But in the City all traces of age were habitually removed by treatments and surgeries that kept people looking as young as possible. So Alistair did not really know what the trace of years really meant. He stared in puzzlement and a little fear at the stooped figure that hobbled toward him bearing weight on a tall, wooden staff.

"That doesn't happen very often," the old man chuckled, looking back at the cave. "Asher going hungry. You must be a clever and resourceful young man."

"Who...who is Asher?" Alistair asked, sharing his

bewildered look from the cave to the old man's wrinkled face and the wild, grey hair that streaked from his head and beard.

"Certainly you met that creature bellowing all that terrible noise," the old man answered. "The one that I'll wager tried to make a meal of you."

"What is he?" Alistair asked, recovering enough from his shock to be curious. "Is that some kind of monster?"

The old man sighed and turned a suddenly mournful stare towards the rising sun.

"Asher used to be one of the most beautiful of earth's creatures," the old man explained. "People would go to him for blessings and cures to their illnesses. Back then the water of the pool was clear and full of light. Pilgrims would crowd this place for a chance to see him, to go winding down those stairs even if just to stand before him.

"You see, then he was not dark yet. It was said to watch him rise up out of the water was joy itself. A strange, but wonderful music would enter your head, lights would dance from his skin and ripple off the water. Some would even claim to see new colors flash before their eyes. No matter what, you would always feel better after you saw him. Sickness, heaviness of heart, broken bones, even broken hearts would be mended by Asher. It was a true wonder to behold. This place was happy then. The grove was full of laughter and life. You can still see the ruins of the old city, just over the hill. It flourished by the business of pilgrims come to see Asher. Now it is all dead."

"What happened?"

Looking at the ground the old man scratched at the grass with his staff. He looked to Alistair as if the question had hurt him.

"Over time people went from loving Asher to worshiping him. They brought him gifts, then praise, then they prayed to him when they weren't even at his pool, believing he could heal from afar. Eventually, all the gifts and praise began to change Asher. He started to demand gifts before he would appear. Whereas before he had given freely. Then he began to employ acolytes to serve him and stewards to control the petitioners that came to him. Before he had welcomed all. Then he made priests to keep sacred fires burning in his honor. His power began to fade as he turned from light to shadow.

"One day he demanded sacrifice, the blood of animals to be spilled for him to devour. He grew darker and fulfilled less. Then one day a poor, young girl came to plead for the life of her baby who had fallen ill. She had brought no sacrifice, and in a fit of rage Asher fell upon her and consumed her. The priests and acolytes fled in horror. A deep darkness fell over the cavern. Asher himself was consumed by the shadow and has hungered ever since. After the first few pilgrims died the people stopped coming. Now he waits for the wayward and the ignorant, ever hungry, scouring the darkness."

"I wonder what could make such a beautiful creature turn dark?" Alistair wondered aloud.

"The people made him into a god," the old man answered. "And when they made him a god they made him a demon."

"Is that what happened to the woman with the wings?" Alistair asked. "The one with all the blue children? She tried to eat me too."

"You escaped Tabitha too," the old man sounded surprised. "You are resourceful and clever.

"But no, Tabitha was not trying to make a meal out of you, but a lover. She would have made love to you until all the warmth was gone from your body and you would have been shrunken and weak just like those children of hers, hunting new, warm lovers for her."

"You mean those blue, glowing creatures were once..."

"Yes, they were men," the old man finished for him. "All of them men who had wandered into Tabitha's grasp and had become her lovers."

"Was her fate like Asher's?" Alistair asked. "Did she turn because she was made into a god?"

"Tabitha has been hunting men long before anyone knew about Asher. Her story goes back further than my lore."

Alistair looked down at his lamp, thankful for the light again. Had he known at the time the peril he faced he doubted his resolve would have held up at all.

"Well you can tell people that light is her weakness," Alistair said holding up the lamp. "All I did was hold this lamp up and she cowered like it burned to look at it."

The old man's eyes widened as he looked at Alistair's lamp. He looked back at Alistair again and a smile broke out over his face.

"Tabitha doesn't mind light at all," he said. "Where did you get this?"

Alistair proceeded to tell his entire story, of how he escaped the city, met up with Bella, had been captured by the High Lord, imprisoned, and finally sentenced to hard labor in the mines. He told of his despair, then his deliverance by the magic lamp, his flight deeper into the earth and the encounters with Tabitha and Asher, although he did not know what he faced at the time.

As Alistair told his story the old man's smile deepened. He looked down again at the lamp and then at Alistair.

"You know, it is not the lamp that is magic," he told him.

"Well of course it is," Alistair said. "This light never goes out, even in wind. Even I can't blow it out, see."

To prove his point Alistair blew a few times right at the flame. The small fire flickered but still burned.

"Yes, I see," the old man agreed. "But the lamp is not magic. Come, I will show you."

***

Alistair followed the old man up the hill and into the forest. They made their way slowly, for they could only walk as fast as the old man's patient gait. And he seemed to be in no hurry, strolling through the forest in perfect leisure. He spoke as he walked, talking of the little white flowers at their feet or the ancient trees that grew around them.

The old man talked also of himself. His name was Adger, and he had been raised as the son of a silversmith. As a young man he took up his father's trade and married a beautiful young woman who had died early in their marriage. The rest of his life he had lived alone, quietly plying his trade in silver craftsmanship.

The path took them out of the forest and up to a little house built into the folds of the hill. Below, the valley was awash in light, and Alistair could see a river running through a wood. For a moment he thought he glanced something bright white dart through the trees, and then a horseman quickly following. He stared down at the valley but caught no other sight of the vision.

"This way, come in," Adger beckoned and Alistair followed him into the cottage.

Inside the cottage was warm and full of books and silver-working instruments and many silver items in various states of completeness. A little fire burned in the hearth, heating a iron pot that hung just over the flames. The old man poured a steaming cup of tea for them both and beckoned for Alistair to sit down.

"You see that candle up there," the old man pointed to a small, tallow candle that burned on the mantle in a humble, tin holder. "Blow that candle out for me."

Alistair stood up and blew at the little candle. The flame sputtered but did not go out. He blew harder with the same result. He blew even harder and all the little flame did was sputter and dance in Alistair's breath.

"You see, that does not go out either," Adger pointed out.

"Is this a magic candle?" Alistair asked.

"It is the not the candle I tell you," the old man laughed. "Just like it is not your lantern that is magic."

"How is it these flames do not go out?" Alistair wondered, still staring at the candle flame.

"It is not the lantern or the candle that is magic," the old man said. "It is the flame."

Alistair stared up at the candle, intrigued by the intrepid, little flame. He held up the lantern that Bella had given him, comparing the two, as if he could see their magical properties himself. But at a glance they just appeared to be regular flames of light.

"Do they have any other power?" Alistair asked. "Besides never going out."

"Well, I should say so!" Adger exclaimed. "Did that light not ward off Tabitha and Asher? Did it not bring you light in the gloom of utter dark? Power indeed! You do not know power, you young people, you men of the city. This light has power beyond your wildest imaginings. The very least I could tell you about. The greatest I will probably never know."

"How did you come about it?" Alistair asked.

The old man smiled and stroked his long beard. A glisten covered his eyes born of fond memories.

"That would be my father," he said. "He had a candle much like that one, and when I was old enough he fashioned one for me and lit it with the light from his own. He told me the light had been passed down for many generations, that we were one of the sacred keepers of the flame. From father to son, for hundreds of years we have passed this flame down. Finally, it has come to me, and I have no son. I feared the flame might be lost when I die...But here you are, and with a flame of your own."

"It's not really my own," Alistair shrugged. "Although I would love to have one of my own."

"Yes, that was given to you," Adger thoughtfully mused. "And it must be given back. This kind of thing can be passed down, but the one who has given this to you needs it back more than she can know. She is, quite literally, lost without it."

"I know," Alistair sighed. "But she is held by the High Lord. I have just escaped him myself."

An incredible sadness came over Alistair as he thought of Bella. He suddenly ached to see her again, to hear her voice. The thought that he might never lay eyes on her again almost made him weep.

"Yes, the High Lord," the old man mused. "He has caused no end of trouble to the land. It would be well for us all if someone were to unseat him."

"Bella told of a legend about him," Alistair remarked. "She said at the end of the Forbidden Road is a weapon that will destroy the High Lord. Do you know of this?"

Adger shrugged. "I have not been to the end of the road myself. Nor do I know much about Rabon, except that he has always had designs on the Lady Bella."

"Designs? Why that is impossible," Alistair laughed.

Alistair recounted the strange things he saw at the High Lord's court. He told how all the ugliest women were considered beauties, especially the hideous Leanna, while Bella, the only true beauty among them, was reckoned ugly.

"That's all part of the plan," the old man explained. "After so many years of demoralizing her, of convincing Bella she is ugly and worthless, when Rabon finally proposes to marry her, out of pity, of course, she will happily leap at the opportunity. Then Rabon will have what she would never have given him willingly."

"Why would Rabon possibly want to do that?" Alistair

asked, sounding more defensive than he liked.

"He wants to be the heir of Bella's fortune," the old man told him. "All that was her father's passed to her, and Rabon wants it."

"He is the High Lord. He has already taken all she owns. What else could he possibly want?"

"There is more to inheritance than gold and land," the old man explained. "Rabon cannot truly control the land until he is Cedric's heir."

After their tea the old man went out back and gathered vegetables from his garden. He mixed them together for a soup and hung the pot over the fire. As they waited he quietly took to his tools and began working.

By the time night fell Adger spooned a bowl of soup for each of them and they ate in silence. After their meal the old man lit a pipe and leaned back, staring into the fire.

"How did the cities get walled up?" Alistair asked his host. "Why aren't we supposed to leave?"

"That is an old story," the old man mused. "It goes back further than my life."

"But do you know?"

"Oh yes, I know," Adger nodded.

The old man fell silent and stared intently into the flames. For a moment Alistair didn't think he would answer his question.

"It began with a war," the old man finally said in a puff of pipe smoke.

"It was quite unlike any war that had ever come before. You see, the world became a divided place, no longer whole as it had been before. It had once been a world of magic and wonder, like a forest full of strange and marvelous things, and also a world of harmony and order. Men built great things and applied his science hand in hand with a mind that recognized the awesome powers that haunt the world. It was a world not untouched by violence and misery, but it was a world in harmony.

"Then something strange happened. Man became divided. He got the foolish notion into his head that faith and magic had no business mixing with reason and science. So he became a divided man, and by results became a smaller one. The world too became divided and grew smaller by result.

"One group of men, who eventually called themselves Moderns, or Realists, believed that only by means of reason and science should men live and conduct his life. They said they were going to disbelieve in anything their eyes couldn't see or their hands couldn't touch. What they really meant is that they would believe only in what they could understand and control. The fact is, they did believe in at least one thing they couldn't see, and that was the progress of science. They didn't know where this progress was heading and did not bother even to ask whether or not this progress was good, only they held devout faith in the infallible march of progress.

"What no one could foresee at the time was that progress and the triumph of science and reason ended up being the creation of the dreary and monotonous city. Because whatever science said must be true, it was true for all. They developed the best clothes for man so everyone wore the same clothes. They developed the most precise way to speak so they demanded that everyone speak the same. They discovered the elements in food most suitable for man's health and built factories that manufactured these foods and declared that men should eat nothing else.

"It was the same with everything. Eventually all men acted the same, talked the same, looked the same, lived in the same type of house, worked the same hours. In short, the progress of science and reason came to mean all men living the same life, productive and safe, but without real joy or any semblance of freedom. They crowded into cities for the sake of efficiency. Then they built walls because they were afraid of what wild things might haunt the forest, things they couldn't understand or control, so they shut them out of sight. Finally, they built all manner of bright lights to shine at all hours. You see, there was nothing these men of reason feared more than the dark. Of all things, reason can never penetrate the mystery of night.

"On the other side were men who believed solely in magic and faith. They loved the mystery of the deep world and all the silent glory of the stars. But they thought that reason was cold and lifeless, the tool of power-hungry and greedy men who desired to rule the world. They called themselves Romantics, and they hated everything the Realists did, whether it was good or not.

"The Romantics refused to live in the city, or have anything to do with it. Instead they lived in the forest and country, at first because they believed that nature was better suited for man than the city. They respected the forest and the hill, even loved it. Over time they began to worship it.

"Because he believed solely in the power of faith and magic, he believed in anything because of faith and magic. Whereas for the Realist there was nothing he would believe in, for the Romantics there was nothing he wouldn't believe in. The Romantics grew more superstitious, refusing to discern anything, accepting all things. They accepted all ways and traditions and philosophies, no matter how contradictory, how foolish, or even how wicked.

"And so the Romantic became lost. His gods would rise and fall with the sun, everyday he found something new to adore. He bowed to this idol, then to another. For the exact opposite reason that life became static in the city, life became static in the country. Romantics refused all progress, and even dreamed of pushing the stream of time until it flowed backwards.

"Things grew more separate until almost all men forgot

how they had become that way. The Realists stayed safe behind their walls long after they had forgotten why the walls were built in the first place. The Romantics worshiped whatever fancy flew into their heads, and were happy as long as fancy was in their heads.

"The great irony is this; that those who professed faith abandoned reason, and in doing so lost all meaningful faith. For faith without reason believes all things, and to believe in everything ultimately means believing in nothing. While reason, devoid of faith and wonder, cannot reason fully, for it only thinks with half its mind.

"But what happened in the country?" Alistair asked when the story was done. "How did the High Lord come to rule?"

"He came from the North somewhere," Adger replied. "No one is quite sure how he came to power or even where he is from. He came promising a new way of life, if the people would just believe in him that he would deliver them all they dreamed. The people wouldn't have to work as hard because his magic would supply most of what they would need. He swore that he could make the ground bring forth more fruit with less effort and the yield would be greater. He promised utopia, a world where man could labor less and possess more.

"But it came with a price. Rabon himself would be lord of everything and everyone. To any mind with sense it became readily apparent that he was only going to deliver on the promise of being a ruler. He was cruel and capricious, seizing whatever he wanted for his personal coffers and for his loyal followers. The rest had to fight for scraps to survive.

"Still, very few resisted. They found it impossible not to believe him. His power was evident, his charm overwhelming, and whenever he wielded his magic most anyone was taken in by whatever foolishness that he promised. Bella's father Cedric was one of the few to resist. He gathered about him all the lords who still had fight within them, that had not been taken in by Rabon's deceptive talk. By then it was too late. One by one they fell until Rabon was the High Lord.

"Cedric was the last to fall as it was. And I believe Rabon hated him more than any other. But he still doesn't truly rule here. His dominion is weak because Cedric was strong and well loved. That's one reason he needs Bella so badly."

A stirring rose up in Alistair at the mention of Bella's plight. He jumped up, full of righteous energy.

"Then we must help her!" he demanded. "We must not let her fall into Rabon's clutches!"

The old man did not respond at first. He continued to stare thoughtfully into the fire.

"Do you hear me?" Alistair asked. "We cannot sit here any longer."

"Yes, but not at the moment," Adger finally answered. "Here, drink first, then we will set out with a plan."

Adger pulled a kettle from over the fire and poured Alistair a steaming cup of tea. Despite Alistair's protests, he was made to drink. The mixture was bitter and hot, but as he drank it became slowly sweeter to his taste.

The old man continued to stare at the fire while Alistair drank the hot tea as quickly as he could. Impatience fumed in him and he itched for action. What action he needed to commit he could not say. He only knew he needed to do something.

Thoughts of the enchanting Bella swam in his brain as he downed the tea and looked into the fire's flames. With her as the last thought on his mind he fell asleep.

"Wake up young man, it is time to move," the old man whispered as he shook Alistair awake.

Alistair looked around, confused and disoriented,

expecting to still be in the darkness of the mine. The fire in the little cabin had gone out and the room was covered in darkness. Adger hovered in his face.

"How long have I been asleep?" Alistair hotly demanded.

"Only a few hours," the old man answered. "Come, you must be off by dawn. We have little time left."

Alistair bolted up and followed the old man who had hurried out the back door.

"Why did we wait, then?" Alistair complained. "We could already have been off by now."

"The darkest of the night is when Rabon is most powerful," Adger explained as the two of them stepped out of the cabin and into the night. "The witching hour is passed and now his power wanes. But we still need the darkness to cover our movement. Now hurry."

The old man guided Alistair down a small road to where a horse, fully packed with wrapped bundles was tethered on a bush. He untied the horse and led him off, urging Alistair to follow. The pale moon rose full and bathed the land in blue light, giving them more than enough to travel by. Still, the old man held Alitsair's lamp up, seeming to only trust in that light.

The pair hurried out of the hills and plunged into a forest. The moonlight was stifled and the glow from the lamp was all that guided them. When they broke out of the trees Adger guided them over the peasant's field, silently creeping among the furrows and the silent tools waiting for the dawn of another work day.

In the distance Alistair saw Rabon's castle. He stopped and stared at the stronghold in the distance, fighting an urge to run right up to it and demand that Bella be given him.

"Come on boy," Adger hissed at him. "You'll do no good to her if you are sent to the mines again. Hurry."

Alistair turned away and followed the old man again.

Their way twisted into a forest again, plunged again into darkness save but the light of the lamp. They traveled quickly, but this forest was vast. Alistair thought he heard whispers all around him. No matter how fast he whipped his head around or how hard he peered into the darkness he could not see their source. Adger seemed not to hear or care, only plunged doggedly through the trees.

When they finally broke out of the woods the sun was beginning to peak over the horizon. Adger stopped and turned around to Alistair.

"We made it," he smiled. "You'll be safe."

Alistair looked around and discovered he was on the road again, the very same road he had set out on upon first leaving the city, the road he knew now to be forbidden. He looked down the way that led back to the city. An odd feeling of homesickness came over him.

"Do you wish to return to the city?" the old man asked, sensing his thoughts. "You know the door is locked. There is no going back once you have left."

Alistair nodded and turned to look down the other way. The path twisted into the woods, winding to places he could not see. This, he knew, was where he must hasten.

"Won't Rabon arrest me again," Alistair noted. "If his soldiers find me they will take me back to him."

"Not so, my boy, not so," the old man smiled and tapped a finger to his head.

"Rabon cannot touch you as long as you stay on the road," Adger confided in him. "That's the secret of the Forbidden Road, why Rabon has forbidden it in the first place. Neither he or his men can touch you. They can threaten and harass you with curses, but as long as you stay on the road they cannot lay a hand on you. Do not forget this.

"The same is true for all the other dangers you will encounter. Your lamp will not save you if you willingly leave the road. Stay on the road no matter what. There are dangers other than Rabon that will seek to destroy you."

Adger reached into the bundle the horse carried and brought out a sword. He stepped up to Alistair and strapped the weapon to him.

"Take this with you if ever you must fight," Adger told him. "But trust the road before any weapon."

Alistair could not help drawing the weapon forth and brandishing it in the new light. A sense of power rushed through him, a thrill that made him feel invincible for a moment.

"Trust the road before any weapon," the old man admonished again, laying a hand on Alistair's arm for emphasis.

Alistair nodded and returned the sword. Adger explained all the other supplies as he showed them where they were packed. In all Adger provided a supply of food, cloaks, travel blankets, a bow and arrows (which Alistair could not figure out), cooking utensils, a knife (tucked quickly into Alistair's waist), a flute (also foreign to Alistair's sight), fire starters, and a device that Alistair did not recognize nor could he determine its use (to us it would look like a golden sundial that fits in the hand).

After showing him his supplies Adger helped the younger man onto the horse and explained what he could about riding.

"What am I to do?" Alistair asked as he was being pushed off.

"Go to the end of the road," the old man instructed. "Find the weapon that is housed there. Then hurry back for Bella. Only you can free the land."

Finally, Adger took the lamp and attached it to a pole that was secured in the saddle so that it hovered in front of the horse.

"Go in the light," Adger blessed with a raised hand.

"And may the light shelter and guide you, may it warm you and bless you, and may you walk always beneath its power."

Alistair thanked the old man and then set off down the road. He turned around after going only a few paces, but the old man was gone.

Once again Alistair was on the road. Where his adventure began his adventure continued. He traveled with a smile and hurried the horse as fast as he dared. But he had not rode for even an hour when he pulled the horse to a stop and stared at the road ahead.

There in a bend in the road, atop a strong and noble destrier, tanned and carved by the sun but still familiar, sat his friend Railing.

* * *

As Alistair was carried off by the guards, thrown into the mines, escaped, helped by the old man Adger, and carried back to the road, Railing had his own adventures and troubles. His, though, were of a different manner and degree altogether.

Once Alistair had been dragged from the room Rabon turned his smile upon Railing. He motioned to the guards and they brought the frightened young man closer to the throne. Railing felt a push on his shoulders and he was forced to his knees.

"I believe you are made of different mettle than your friend," Rabon said as he leaned towards Railing.

"Come, you can be honest, you were deceived by your friend. I know you are not like him at all."

Railing looked nervously at the door behind him. A sense of dread for his friend rose up from the pit of his stomach. Even the thought of betraying him made him feel sick.

"Don't worry about your friend," Rabon said as if

reading Railing's troubled thoughts. "We are doing him a favor. Believe me, it is for the best that we drive the poetry out of him. It will only lead to trouble and disaster. Allow me to be good to you."

Railing did not answer at first. He lifted his eyes to meet Bella's. He could see the pain etched across her face. A resolve rose up in him to not submit to any kindness the High Lord might offer.

"Do what you will to me," he uttered. "I will not betray my friend. The fault for leaving the city is as much mine as his."

A loud laugh came bellowing from Rabon. He almost fell back in his chair and slapped his leg. The court immediately joined in, though forced, as if they had no idea what was so amusing.

"I like that courage," Rabon finally said. "What nobility. And that's exactly why you are here and your friend has been sent to the mines.

"I am only trying to help him, you must believe me. That is my job, to be a father to all my people. You cannot know this, but to be consumed by poetry is one of the most awful things that can happen to a man. It dissolves all practicality from him. He will spend his days dreaming and his nights staring at the stars. He becomes full of sighs and imaginary misery. He can do no work because his mind wanders like a listless wind. What good is such a man? What could he contribute to society? I must root this out of your Alistair. Then he can re-enter society, and fully rehabilitated, become a productive member of the community."

"You plan to release him?" Railing asked suspiciously, not daring to believe what Rabon said, but not possessing enough duplicity in his own heart to believe that there was deceit in others.

"Of course," Rabon chuckled. "I have no hate for Alistair. I only want him healed. You know how dreamy he can be."

The High Lord's words made sense to Railing. It was certainly true that Alistair was given to sighs and dreaming. He remembered how just that night in their prison Alistair stared at the moonlight and seemed to be on the verge of tears. And he did talk about how terrible his work had been and that it was impossible to concentrate for all the longing that plagued his heart.

"What are your plans for me?" Railing asked.

"Ah, for you I have just the thing," Rabon smiled. "Bring me Craddock!"

Almost immediately a grizzled, bearded man stepped up beside Rabon's throne. He looked Railing up and down, appraising him with a thoughtful eye. He looked at Rabon and nodded his approval, satisfied with whatever he saw.

"This is Craddock," Rabon offered by way of introduction. "He is the Master of the Hunt. Would you like to learn to hunt?"

"I don't know," Railing answered. "I have never hunted before."

"Oh, I think this is exactly what fits you Railing," Rabon said with a smile. "To hunt is to chase down the plains of the world. You will ride as free as the wind. You will be master of the outdoors, feared by everything that moves, proficient in many weapons. To hunt is to chase and conquer. I believe it will suit you well."

As Rabon spoke Railing felt his heart stir. His mind seemed to open wide and he could feel the wind on his face and the thrill of the chase. Indeed, Rabon had seen truly and knew that the heart that beat in Railing's breast was the heart of a hunter.

From that day Railing came under the tutelage of the grizzled Craddock. Though the Hunt Master rarely spoke, Railing felt an affinity towards him. Whenever words passed through the wild shock of beard were meaningful and important.

Everyday Railing received instruction in hunting. In the morning they practiced weapons, bow and arrow and spear primarily, but they were endless varieties of each. After lunch he learned tracking and reading the signs of animal's passage and habit. Later in the afternoon they practiced riding.

Railing took to all of his lessons with natural ability. Within a few days he had become proficient in the bow, deadly with seven varieties of spear, a master on the horse and an expert in finding the traces of even the smallest game.

At night, as his muscles joyfully ached with weariness, he was invited to Rabon's court. At first he stayed on the outside of the crowd, feeling intensely guilty that he enjoyed himself so much while Alistair suffered in the dark of the mines. He hated the effeminate courtiers, despising their pale weakness as he grew stronger and more colored by the sun everyday. But as the nights passed his guilt began to subside and he thought less and less of his unfortunate friend.

Although he sat every night among the company of the courtiers, Railing never mixed in their company. Most of the time he spent staring out the window, down at the plains of the night, wishing he was out there instead of trapped inside. Other times he would walk through the castle, wandering along the parapets and wishing he were set free into the outdoors. For although he was given freedom around the castle, Railing still had the feeling he was a prisoner.

Finally the day came when Craddock determined Railing was ready for his first hunt. They rose early that morning, packed and mounted while the mists of night still swirled around them. Just as the sun fully peaked over the horizon, a band of twelve hunters, led by Craddock, rode out over the plains.

As soon as they left the castle Railing felt his heart soar

like it never had before. He laughed out loud and couldn't repress the whoop that screamed from his lips. The feel of the horse beneath him, the thrill of his speed, the wind and the dawn coursing through him all pulsed through his veins and lifted his soul on the heights of ecstasy. It was the kind of joy a man feels when he experiences for the first time the very thing he was made to do.

The hunters rode out over the plains and plunged into a deep forest. Craddock followed a trail that Railing could only barely make out. Every once and a while he caught glimpses of an animal's passing, but nothing more than hints. After an hour they rested the horses and then continued on.

For most of the morning the hunters followed the sparse trail. About midmorning they burst out of the forest and out onto a new plain. Below them lay a large and fertile valley. And in the midst of the vale below ran a herd of deer.

The thrill that drove Railing increased its intensity until he thought he could not sit still in the saddle. His quarry was in sight.

"Weapons up," Craddock instructed.

Railing knew by the look of the animal just the weapon to use. He pulled out his bow and nocked the proper sized arrow. The hunters fanned out and began a slow trot down the valley.

The hunters trotted until the herd began to stir. Down below they could see the restlessness pick up and soon the animals would stampede. All at once the hunters spurred the horses into a gallop. Railing squeezed his horse with his thighs to steady himself, hardly able to wait until they were in striking distance.

The charge became a thrill and a blur for Railing. When they reached bow shot of the herd the deer were in full panic. His first shot went wild, falling harmlessly to the ground. His second likewise fell short. For his third shot he forced himself steady, shut out all thoughts except the pull of the hunt that drew him on. He aimed and shot, the arrow burying deep into the flesh of a young buck.

As the buck fell Railing let out another whoop of joy. He quickly nocked another arrow and fell back into the stampeding herd. He hit some and missed many, but never felt more alive as he darted through the fleeing animals, never more a master of his world as then.

When the herd had finally scattered away the hunters returned to gather their trophies. All in they had slaughtered nearly thirty animals with many more injured and hobbled away. They gathered the bodies together and attached the travois to the horses. They piled the bodies on and rode back to the castle, each man dragging behind his share of the kill.

When they arrived back at the castle the servants ran out to unload the kill and begin processing the prizes for the lord and his entourage. Railing sighed as he dismounted and began to make his reluctant way back to the castle. Craddock threw an arm around his neck and pulled him close.

"You made your first kill," the grizzled huntsman grinned and told him. "You don't have to spend another night with those perfumed dandies. You're a hunter now. You stay with us."

The other hunters cheered as Craddock steered Railing into the crowd. They all congratulated him, slapped his back and roughly welcomed him into their company. Railing eagerly let himself be admitted to the inner circle and taken through the castle grounds to the streets of the outside village. He couldn't have been happier.

The hunters made their way through the village to an inn called The King of Harts. A deer with an unusually large spread of antlers graced the wooden placard swinging over the door. Inside, the common room buzzed with life; men drinking and singing songs, a fire roaring warmth from the far wall, young women laughing among the men and others dancing to the tune of a bawdy song.

Most of the night Railing could not help but smile. He had never remembered feeling more at home in a place in his life. The thrill from the hunt still burned in his blood, and his fellow hunters did not stop toasting him and pushing tankards of dark, rich ale into his hands. Railing felt that he was at last in the company of his brothers.

Throughout the night Railing drank and learned the songs the people sang. The hunters told stories of past exploits, tales daring, funny and full of life like Railing had never known. A redheaded woman, young and fiery, glanced his way brazenly as the night wore on. The men all noticed and egged Railing on with crude jokes and taunts. As the men became drunk and drifted away the redhead remained, hardly allowing him out of her sight. Her eyes remained fixed on him and Railing began to believe he could feel her heat from across the room.

When the night wore thin Railing stumbled over to the redhead and said things to her he couldn't remember the day after. She smiled at him and stroked his face. He couldn't help but drink in the way she looked at him, as if he were the strongest and most handsome man in creation. He followed her upstairs and they shared their love together. A contented sleep fell over him as he lay next to the redhead woman whose name he did not know.

* * *

Railing dreamt of the white doe again. He stood with his crowd of hunters on the rise of a hill. It was the very same scene he had dreamed at Bella's cottage. This time he recognized the men around him, his fellow hunters. This time the hunting spear in his hand felt familiar.

He looked down at the elk grazing in the valley below. Although they dominated the grassland he also recognized deer, moose, bison, boar and hare sharing the fertile land. It was as if every good animal to hunt gathered together below them. He could feel the excitement of the men around him.

Suddenly in the midst of the animals he spied the white doe, pure and lovely, dancing among the lesser animals like a graceful queen moving among clumsy and dirty peasants. The other hunters saw her too and the party drove down into the valley, eager for the prize kill.

All of the hunters went straight for the white doe. They fired arrows and launched their spears. The deer danced through them effortlessly, darting among the other animals. She looked to Railing as if she enjoyed the hunt as much as the hunters.

Railing did not release his weapons as the others did. He kept his spear couched as he chased the doe, watching as she darted back and forth, learning the way she moved.

Just as the doe broke out of the herd Railing let his spear fly. His aim was true and the point dug deep into the doe's flesh. The animal fell as a red stain spread out over the flawless, white hide. Railing opened his mouth to scream in celebration when a pain ripped through his own heart.

Railing tumbled to the ground, the breath ripped from his lungs. He grasped at his throat, terrified how his breath had left him. The pain in his heart spasmed and jerked, filled him with dread and nausea.

He rolled over and his eyes met those of the wounded doe. For a moment he thought he could see humanity in those eyes, something deep and sad. He wept as the pain tore through him. And as consciousness began to fade he saw tears rolling from the doe's eyes.

Life as a hunter was perfect for Railing. At least every other day the hunting party mounted up early in the morning and drove out in search of game. Sometimes they hunted just for the day, other times they camped out and spent days chasing distant herds. These were the best times for Railing. He would sleep under the stars and gaze up at heaven as exhaustion rolled over him, almost feeling guilty at how content he felt. If the moon was out he would look up at her and wonder if anything in the world was more beautiful.

There was very little that the hunters did not seek out. Whatever Lord Rabon's appetite desired the party would hunt. Sometimes it was simply venison of one sort or another, but also bison or hare. Often it was pheasant or goose or wild turkey. The hunter's favorite was when the request for wild hog came in and they tracked down the deadly boar.

Dreams of the white doe began to haunt Railing almost daily. Little details in the dream changed. Sometimes he killed the doe in the herd, sometimes he chased her into the forest. He usually killed her with his hunting spear, other times an arrow felled her. But the major features remained the same. He always found her in a herd of varying animals. She always managed to elude the other hunters. He always killed her, and when he did, he felt the same pain that he delivered, as if he were wounded by his own weapon.

The days not spent hunting were used to train and exercise and await Lord Rabon's pleasure. Nights when they weren't camping on the hunt they spent at the King of Harts, drinking, singing and sharing stories. Sometimes Railing would stay with the redhead, sometimes he would sleep in the common room of the inn. If he cared to he would stumble back to the castle and sleep there. Other women would throw themselves at the hunters. Some nights Railing would enjoy their pleasures too. The redhead didn't seem to mind.

One night another hunter limped into the common room. He was unfamiliar to Railing, but he walked with an air of undeniable self-assurance despite the lame leg that moved stiffly. Craddock jumped up in recognition, ran across the inn and wrapped the man up in an affectionate embrace. The two greeted each other warmly and Craddock pulled him over to where the hunters gathered.

"Boys, I want you to meet the best hunter that has ever stalked game," Craddock gushed with introduction. "This is Erin the Hawk, a king among men."

Erin sat down with the other hunters and took his drink. The tales immediately began to spin around the table. Craddock and Erin laughed and bragged and reminisced about exploits past. They talked about their finest hunts and worst failures, and even told the story of how Erin had his leg crushed by an elk. The reason for his limp to that day.

As Erin the Hawk remembered with the other hunters, Railing could not help but notice a sadness around the old hunter's grey eyes. Even as he laughed at their old misadventures, the laughter never touched his eyes. It seemed to Railing that the Hawk carried an old grief, a wound as deep as his shattered leg, and no amount of happiness could cure him.

"So, are you still on your great hunt?" Craddock finally asked as the empty cups littered the table late into the night.

"Aye, I still search for the herd," Erin answered, the sadness in his eyes growing darker.

An uncomfortable silence fell upon the table. The usually jubilant hunters looked at each other, their unease plainly visible.

"So what is this herd?" Railing had to ask.

Craddock and Erin exchanged a meaningful glance. The one grinned while the other stared darkly.

"Go on, you tell him," Craddock finally said. "It's your bloody fantasy."

If Erin was offended he didn't show it.

"Keep telling yourself that, Craddock," Erin retorted. "You know better. You saw for yourself."

"You don't know what I saw," Craddock retorted, anger edging his voice. "And for that matter you don't know what you saw either. None of us did that day. Don't tell me what

I saw."

"I can't fool myself as easy as you," Erin said as he looked into his empty cup. "I know what I saw."

"You're one to talk the fool," Craddock huffed and turned his own drink up, slamming the empty cup on the table.

The two men stared each other down. Some unspoken secret, fermented into animosity silently passed between them. Eventually Erin shrugged and turned to Railing.

"The herd we are talking about is the Great Herd," Erin told him. "The herd of Alvalon, the Hunter King."

As Erin spoke the other hunters leaned eagerly in to listen. Even the sullen Craddock was cowed into a reverent silence. Railing felt as if the secrets of the hunter's lore were being opened to him.

"As the legend goes, the Hunter King gathers for himself all the biggest and most beautiful animals in all the world's forests. But not only that, they have to be the most elusive and daring and capable of escaping the cleverest of hunters. It doesn't matter what kind of game animal it is, he takes them all: grouse, pheasant, deer, elk, caribou, boar, duck, geese, hare, whatever is worthy to hunt he keeps.

"Now only the finest are what he desires. After an animal has fully grown, evaded hunters for years, become a legend around the parts that he haunts, only then does the Hunter king finally take him as his own, granting the animal immortality as part of his herd. It's the highest honor for an animal and a hunter's greatest challenge. It's even been said that to slay one of the Hunter King's quarry brings with it a favor that can be asked of the king, a reward for doing what none other could do. Thousands of hunters have searched for Alvalon's Herd and the best have only returned with legends and hearsay."

"But if it is a whole herd how hard can it be to track?" Railing asked, fascinated already at the prospect of hunting the herd himself.

"But don't you see, this is no ordinary herd," Erin leaned in to explain. "Not only are these animals the cleverest of their kind, as a part of the herd they are given magical protection. They can't be seen under normal conditions."

"There are only two times you can see them or their tracks," Craddock joined in. "At dawn and dusk. You have a brief opportunity, less than an hour as the sun falls or rises. Then they disappear, tracks and all. Just like that you can't find so much as a mouse dropping."

"Every so often you hear of a shepherd being scared out of his mind as a massive herd of prize animals comes thundering past as he shivers in the dawn," Erin added. "Or a fisherman coming in for the night sees them grazing on the far hills and then fade with fall of dark."

"But there is one other time the herd can be seen," Erin said.

"Bah, that is as pointless as the others," Craddock waved him off.

"At an eclipse," Erin continued. "When the sun fades dark or the moon turns blood red, the herd can be seen and tracked.

"But no one knows when that will happen," Craddock shrugged. "What good will it do you?"

"I talked with an astronomer two weeks ago," Erin excitedly said. "A man with a reputation for predicting all sorts of celestial wonders, learned in the knowledge of the ancient ones. He told me that three days from now will be one such moment, the sun will turn black and night will fall in the middle of the day."

Another silence fell over the hunter's table. This one rich with possibility and unspoken hope. Craddock was the first to break it.

"You assume we believe that crazy legend enough to care," he huffed.

"I know you believe it," Erin shrugged, drinking from a new draft of beer.

"We don't know what we saw," Craddock argued. "The light was bad, it was a flash and then it faded before our very eyes. Gone like it never was there. I don't know what I saw. A trick of the sun."

"That may be true but for one thing," Erin said as he pointed a finger at Craddock. "We both saw the white doe."

Railing felt his blood run cold. Images flashed in his head, resurrected dreams of a flawless doe dodging through the herd, the wound he inflicts and his own searing pain. The idea that what he dreamed could be true was almost too much for his earth-bound mind to manage.

"Aye, I did see her," Craddock reluctantly agreed, his shoulders slumping in resignation. "And never have I seen such a perfect animal, standing in the mist of the dawn, turned to us, a queen among the beast. I could tell she was their queen. There was no doubt of that. She was flawless, I swear she was."

"The white doe is the prize of Alvalon's herd," Craddock explained to Railing. "Legend says she lived in a duke's hunting ground for ten years, hunted every day, and never a spear came near her side. She is without doubt the most beautiful of all those beautiful creatures. If any hunter were to master her as a trophy he would be a legend forever. Although it is said that to kill her would induce Alvalon's wrath, so deeply does he cherish the animal. But there isn't a hunter alive that wouldn't risk it all and more for just a single spear throw at her. I know I would die happy."

"But at the end of the day it's just talk," Craddock continued. "Even with the eclipse in that doesn't help us. It would take months to even find the herd."

"I've been hunting them for twenty years," Erin told them solemnly, the weariness suddenly apparent in his voice. "Just this sunset today I saw traces of the Great Herd not two miles from here. I couldn't resist coming by. It's the chance of a lifetime, Craddock, for all of you. The opportunity doesn't get any better, and you know it."

Craddock put up a weak argument for the better part of an hour. It was obvious to everyone he would go. The hunters themselves were practically on fire, burning with eagerness. To even take part in chasing Alvalon's herd is a tale in itself. To actually see it would be legendary. That's as far as any of them dared think.

Railing was the only one frightened. The dream terrified him even as it thrilled him. He heard little of the argument around him. He was vaguely aware of Craddock's final agreement. He heard distantly the plan to leave that next morning before sunrise so they could find fresh traces of the herd. He barely noticed his own feet taking him to a room upstairs where he fell asleep, haunted again by dreams of the white doe.

* * *

The next morning, when dark still covered the world, Railing rode out with the band of hunters, now led by Erin as well as Craddock. They made quick time to Erin's last mark, and as dawn crept up they could all make out signs of a great herd that had passed through, tracks that no hunter could miss, so great was the size of the herd.

Without hesitation Erin rode off, desperate to follow the trail in the fading dawn. They rode hard as the sun drew closer to the horizon. The light grew brighter and Railing noticed the signs of passage grow dimmer and dimmer. It was as if the marks he saw on the ground were made of mist and a mere breath of wind would blow them away.

When the sun finally peeked over the rim of the world, the last, dim trace of the herd disappeared. The hunters found themselves staring at ground that looked as clean and undriven as freshly fallen snow. The party slowed down, unable to go any further.

"We have to split off from here," Erin told the party as he pulled up. "We spread out a league apart and keep riding. When the sun sets one of us should see signs of the herd again unless they turn completely around. Once the sun goes down and you see sign of the herd blow your horn, we'll come to you."

The hunters split off and formed a line, each rider a league from the other. All day long they rode, not driving their horses hard but putting up a good pace. As soon as the sun fell Railing began to look for signs of the trail again. He had barely put his head down when the sound of a hunter's horn rose in the distance.

Railing pressed his mount and rode towards the sound. It sounded again, changing direction and drawing quickly away. Railing steered towards the sound, loving every second of the rush through the darkening forest.

Railing caught up with the hunter who had sounded the horn and most of the party had already joined him. The sun had faded and the trail had died with the dusk.

"Good things happened today boys," Erin flushed with excitement as he flew off his horse. "We're fresh on the trail and getting closer, I can smell it I swear!"

They camped that night under the stars, Railing drifting off to sleep with a smile on his face. Just as he fell completely into unconsciousness thoughts of his friend Alistair leapt into his mind. A twinge of guilt followed, that he should be so deeply enjoying himself while his friend suffered. But then he saw the moon rising and couldn't find it in himself to be miserable, whether for his sake or another's.

As dawn rose the next day signs of Alvalon's herd materialized with the light. They rode hard in pursuit, taking quick advantage of the failing dawn. Like the day before they split off when the trail vanished and rode apart, hoping that one of the hunters would still be on the trail when dusk fell.

For the next two days the hunters pursued their prey in this manner. When they were certain of the trail they rode hard, following the obvious signs in the scant light. During the day they rode slower, lest they erred and would be forced to backtrack.

The hunter's luck was with them, Erin had said. Every night they slept hot on the herd's trail. Both he and Craddock grew visibly excited as the other hunters showed signs of that peculiar anxiety when one is terrified and thrilled all at once.

On the third day, just before the sun rose, Erin stood alone as the other hunters stirred awake. He paced the camp, eager to be in the saddle. As soon as dawn showed signs of the elusive herd he tore off down the trail.

They followed as far as they could, then split off again. But before they split off Erin spoke to the group.

"This is the day boys," he rubbed his hands together and said. "The wise man told me the eclipse would last three hours from start to finish. When the moon touches the sun you should be able to see the trail appear, then ride like the devil and blow your horn like the dark one is on your heels. Mount up boys!"

Railing could not help but glance up at the sky from time to time, watching the moon creep closer to the sun. A few hours after midday he felt an odd sensation wash over him. He felt as if the world was turning, as if there was suddenly something wrong that he couldn't explain. He glanced up at the sky and saw the moon covered in shadow, just touching the rim of the sun.

Immediately the ground shifted underneath him and Railing could see a swath of churned and trampled earth. He stood right over the path of the great herd. He gave three sharp blasts to his horn and flew off in pursuit.

Railing couldn't tell how long he rode. His horse lathered and sweat and trembled beneath him but he kept pushing the mount, knowing the urgency of their hunt. Just as dark fell over the land, when the moon moved over to block out almost all of the sun's light, Railing rode up over a ridge and pulled suddenly up short. There, in a broad valley beneath him grazed Alvalon's legendary herd.

For a moment all Railing could do was stare in amazement. At least one of every animal he knew stirred in the valley below. There seemed to be hundreds more he didn't recognize, strange beasts that were of odd shapes, spotted, decorated with twisting horns or leathery hides of skin. But one thing they all had in common was the extraordinary beauty of them all.

He had barely time to drink the sight in when the rest of the hunters rode up to join him. Something akin to jealousy rose in Railing, a feeling that he wanted to keep all of these majestic animals to himself. Perhaps he even entertained the idea that these animals were too beautiful to kill, that the rare spectacle of their unique splendor was made to be enjoyed. For a moment Railing regretted he was a hunter.

"Would you look at it boys," Erin said all breathless as he paused on the crest of the hill. "Aye Craddock? More wonderful than I remember."

All Craddock could do was nod as he stared speechless down at the legendary herd. All of the hunters seemed to be frozen in amazement, looking at a living myth before them. Railing even hoped that their hesitation would mean they wouldn't hunt at all. Surely something so beautiful as these creatures should be allowed to live, he thought. He could even see that the mere fact of being alive was most of their beauty.

"Hunters, to me!" Erin cried out, breaking the spell cast over the men.

With a cry the hunters spread out and charged down the

hill towards the valley. Railing followed reluctantly. Though he couched his spear and cried as loud a jubilation as the others, he did so with only half his heart.

Still he sped down the valley with the others. He watched them charge the herd that seemed not to notice at first. Then that first head shot up in alarm, the body tensed suddenly. Like a preternatural instinct a few others sensed the first animals panic and looked up and saw the charging horsemen. The first animals nimbly scattered away, and then all at once the stampede began.

Railing watched his fellow hunters with no intention of casting a spear. Erin was the first to throw, followed quickly by Craddock's hurl. Both spears fell short. They drew reserves and hurled again, these too missed. The other hunters launched their own spears, and all of them missed their mark.

When Erin had thrown all of his spears he unslung his bow and began to fire arrows into the herd. Railing could see an intense frustration on the hunter's face as even his arrows missed. The animals did not even seem to be trying to avoid the missiles. They moved without effort, cutting one way then the other, changing direction just as the hunters threw their spears, but seemingly unaware of anything but the charge of the stampede.

Railing had not hurled a single shot. He rode with the hunters amid the retreating herd, amazed at how the animals deftly avoided their pursuers. He felt an even deeper admiration for the animals, their natural beauty and the way they danced in magical elusiveness. As he rode he began to feel a strange disorientation, as if he were more a part of the herd than one of the hunters.

A white flash danced out of the corner of his vision. He whipped his head around and froze to see a white doe dancing through the charging herd. She appeared just as in his dream, though her real beauty far eclipsed the vision.

Without doubt she was the most perfect animal he had ever seen.

Railing charged towards the doe, pushing his horse to keep up with the nimble creature. He swerved through the herd, nearly crashing into animals larger than his horse. She drew him through the herd, out towards the edge of the stampede and suddenly stopped.

Railing drew up his spear with every intent of letting loose. But he stopped. The dream rose up in his mind and he dared not throw. The doe simply stared at him. Something strange about her luminous eyes bore into Railing's soul. He relaxed and let his spear drop knowing there was no way he could kill the animal.

The doe turned and plunged into the forest, leaving the herd behind. Without thinking Railing charged after the deer, hardly hearing the cries of warning from the hunters behind him.

As soon as he plunged into the shadow of the trees a strange feeling washed over him. The shadows felt darker, the patches of sunlight somehow brighter, the green of the leaves more verdant and rich, and even the sound of the forest beneath him sharper and more crisp. It was as if all of his senses suddenly acquired a greater clarity. At the same time Railing had the undeniable feeling that he had crossed some perilous threshold, or stepped through a doorway into another world, though by appearance, everything seemed the same.

He could not pause to wonder at the sudden change. Railing saw the doe disappear down a trail and he pressed in after her. Without even caring where he went he charged to the hunt. Something in the back of his mind warned him that he was plunging into danger, but he found he had little concern for it. And even his lack of concern frightened him. But he charged on.

Time seemed to lose its effect on Railing as he chased the

doe. He became dimly aware of night falling, dark and moonless, but he chased without needing much light at all. He felt the morning rise again and hardly noticed it. Fatigue did not touch him, or apparently his mount either. They both hunted without the burden of any of their limitations.

The sun set and rose again. Then it set and rose a third time. Still Railing chased the doe through forests he did not know. For a moment he would close his pursuit, sometimes so near he could catch the doe's scent, strangely aromatic, like a blend of empyrean flowers. Then she would dart away beyond his sight. Other times he only caught flashes of white through the darkness and press his pursuit in hope alone.

The dreamy hunt continued until one dusk, on the edge of the fourth sunset since the chase began, the deer paused on the banks of a river. Railing got off his tireless mount, spear in hand again and approached on foot. He crept closer and the doe looked at him again. Railing didn't even bother to lift the spear. The doe turned and dove into the river.

The spell over Railing's mind suddenly broke. For the first time in days he felt like himself again. He shook the torpor from his head and looked around, half-amazed at where he was, and ran to the bank of the river.

From the bank Railing could see the doe swimming across. She ducked beneath the surface so only a ripple across the slowly moving waters marked her passage. He squinted in the failing light, straining to watch her movement, afraid he might finally lose his quarry.

The water broke and the doe began to emerge on the far bank. But instead of the white doe, a woman rose from the waters. The breath caught in Railings lungs as she turned and looked at him. The dusk glimmered off the water that beaded down her naked skin. He felt paralyzed beneath the gaze of her dark eyes. She regarded him silently, unashamed of her nakedness. He moved his eyes freely over her body, feeling the curve of her hips, the smoothness of her muscular legs, the swell of her breasts, even touching the dark, wet hair with the power of vision alone. He had never been smitten before, but in that moment Railing felt the immovable force of love batter his soul.

As if she knew what he felt the woman smiled and turned away, running up the far bank. Railing dove into the river, unwilling to lose sight of her now, even if he must swim across the ocean to get her. He swam to the far bank and ran up to the forest, chasing the woman on his own feet.

He had run barely a mile when a lodge appeared in the woods ahead. The door was closing with a naked foot retreating quickly inside, and Railing knew it was the woman he sought. But he didn't charge immediately in. For a moment his attention was caught by the lodge in front of him.

The building looked to be as large as Rabon's castle. Instead of stone this structure was made of piled timbers topped by a thatch roof. Round windows cut into the walls, as well as dormers and balconies. The lodge seemed extremely complex for all its simplicity of material.

Railing walked cautiously to the front door and found it easily pulled open at his touch. The inside was lit generously with torches, lining a long hallway. He could see well enough to make out the roof timbers above and the walls covered in trophies as far as the eye could see. Every once and a while he would pass doors off to the side, but for some unexplained reason he knew they weren't for him.

The long hallway finally ended. Another door faced Railing, one that felt right. He ducked inside it and found himself in a small room, warm and cozy, heated by a blazing fire.

"Welcome hunter," a deep and soothing voice called out.

Railing turned and saw an older man, but not old enough to be considered aged, sitting in a chair by the fire. His long beard sprouted from every direction out of a worn and swarthy face. The man was wrapped in furs and stretched a large hand towards Railing.

"Come in, warm yourself by the fire," he welcomed.

Railing moved towards the fire and saw the woman he had chased sitting beside the older man. She was clothed now, but her dark eyes gazed into his heart, reminding him of the unadorned beauty he had seen earlier. If anything she was more beautiful now, as the fire cast a strange light over her face and her body close enough for him to touch though he dared not.

"Sit," the older man instructed.

Railing sat down by the fire. The woman rose and began to serve him. She handed him a plate of roasted meat and a mug of beer. When she leaned in towards him he drank in her scent, the smell of exotic flowers that he had caught while on her trail. She stared deep into him as her braid fell down and brushed his face and he trembled with excitement, and could even feel her though she did not touch him.

He ate and drank and could hardly keep his eyes off the woman. From time to time he had to force himself to regard the older man out of respect. The bearded figure only smiled when he did so, as if he knew a secret that Railing did not, which for certain he did. Once Railing had finished his food the woman brought him another beer and a mug for herself and the older man.

"Do you know who I am?" the older man asked, wiping foam from his wild moustache.

"You are Alvalon, the Hunter King," Railing said, certain of his guess.

"I am," the Hunter King smiled and drank deeply from his mug of beer.

"And do you know my daughter?"

"I am certain I don't," Railing answered. "For I know I would remember such a woman. I have never seen her equal."

"She is Nivena," Alvalon told him. "And she has found you most worthy of her attention."

Railing couldn't help but steal a look at the Hunter King's daughter. She blushed and looked away from him. In that simple movement he found her more enchanting than ever.

"I can't imagine anything I have done to earn such an honor," Railing said, still not able to take his eyes off of Nivena.

"You are a true hunter," Alvalon told him. "Your heart was found whole. You passed every test that a truly great hunter must face."

"There was no test," Railing protested. "There is nothing I did to deserve the honor of your daughter's attention."

Nivena smiled up at Railing, filled with pleasure at Railing's speech.

"But you were tested," the Hunter King insisted. "You showed yourself skilled in all the ways of hunting when you found the herd. You showed yourself persistent and strong when you chased the white doe for three days, passing into the hunter's ecstasy, not feeling the passage of time or distance or succumbing to weariness. Only a true hunter could accomplish that.

"And most importantly, twice you had the opportunity to slay an animal from my herd and you did not loose your spear; once when you were riding among the herd, and a second time when the white doe was cornered by the river. Tell me, why didn't you try for the kill?"

"I don't know," Railing said, suddenly embarrassed. "I guess my heart failed me and I couldn't bring myself to kill any of your animals. Such a weakness should tell you how undeserving I am."

"Not so, hunter," Alvalon laughed. "In fact, you proved your heart to be true by not slaying any of my animals.

"You see, a true hunter does not need to slaughter all that

he sees. If he is true he can see the beauty of a creature and admire it for a living thing. Some animals are too noble to be taken as trophies. That's why they are in my herd. The men you hunt with have no such vision. All they can see is glory for themselves. They are blind to the beauty of their prey. But you can see them truly and so did not wish to kill them."

Railing thought back to when he stood on the crest of the hill and stared in admiration at the beautiful animals grazing below. He knew the Hunter King spoke truly. He remembered too the other hunters trying to slay the animals of the herd but all their attempts failing.

"The other hunters, though skilled that they are, could not kill any of your herd. All of their best attempts missed."

"That is the reward of being in my herd," Alvalon told him. "There is no mortal man that can kill them now. These are creatures not to be trophies, but admired for their beauty and strength."

Up to this point Nivena had not spoken a word. Her dark eyes would fix upon Railing, then at the fire. Always that strange and intoxicating smile graced her features, churning and melting the guts inside of him.

"I am honored by such attention," Railing told his host. "But I would hear the favor of the lady from her own lips. To do so would be death and life for me."

"That you cannot do," Alvalon told him. For the first time Nivena looked sad and the smile fell from her face.

"You may hear her sing, but she cannot speak. Not until a worthy man has pledged his life to her will her voice be loosened and she possess the powers of normal speech."

"If you find me worthy then I will make that pledge this very night," Railing vowed as he leapt from his chair.

Oh, there are many ways I find you worthy, hunter," Alvalon said. "There is but one that I don't."

"Tell me how I am unworthy and I will amend it right away," Railing swore, his blood running hot with the thought of Nivena as his own.

The Hunter King sighed and shook his head. He reached a fatherly hand to his daughter who looked back up at him with a knowing smile.

"For many years we have been waiting for a man worthy of my daughter, one who can give her a true voice. At night she sings the saddest songs, waiting for the one that will free her. And you, hunter, have come near to being that one. There is but the question of your honor."

"What ever does that mean?!" Railing spat indignantly. "What stain is there on my honor?!"

"Is there not a friend of yours languishing in the prison of the mines as we speak?" Alvalon reminded him. "While you have been living a life of carelessness and hunting he has suffered mightily. Was he not a true friend? And yet you flourish as he withers? Where is your honor there? Where is your conscience?"

Railing fell back into the chair, dejected and ashamed. Tears welled up from deep inside of him, a place that groaned and ached. He dropped his head into his hands and wept. He wept for the only friend he had ever had in life, and the only one he had ever betrayed.

"You are right," Railing cried, unable to look either Alvalon or Nivena in the face. "I am unworthy of even your pity, wretch that I am. Alistair is a true friend, and I have been giddy on the hunt while he suffers for us both."

"Hold your tears," Alvalon comforted him. "They will not help your friend. You may be worthy yet."

"How can I help him?" Railing asked desperately. "I am but one man and Rabon is the lord of a vast nation. He has magic and powers beyond my own. What can I do?"

"Rabon is but one man also," the Hunter King reminded him. "He can die like any other."

"How can I best him? It is said that no ordinary weapon can kill him."

"At the end of the Forbidden Road is a weapon that Rabon is powerless against," Alvalon said. "Find that weapon and you will have the power to overthrow him."

Railing tried to rise, to leave immediately on a quest to find the road again, when an incredible exhaustion overcame him. His head swam and he fell back into the chair.

"Be still hunter," Alvalon soothed him. "The ecstasy is wearing off and your exhaustion returns. For three days you have been without rest. Come with us and find sleep."

Nivena rose and helped Railing to his feet. He stumbled but her strength held him up. Leaning on her they followed her father up a long stair and onto the roof of his lodge. Nivena lowered him onto a couch, and as she leaned over him he drank in her scent and his body ached to touch hers.

A parade of stars blazed overhead. The sight brought a surge of energy through Railing's tired body. Never before had he seen so many lights move in the heavens above him. A strange stirring moved through his heart, much like the feeling he had for Nivena, but coming from a deeper place.

Nivena put a cup into his hands. He drank deeply and tasted something thick and sweet, flavored in spices and fruit. He felt warmth spread through his body and a sudden contentment. Nothing felt better at that point than to lay embraced in the couch and watch the stars overhead.

The presence of the Hunter King stirred nearby and settled into a couch beside Railing. He heard Nivena also seated on the other side of him.

"You see those stars up there," the Hunter King pointed out a particular group of stars. "The ones that lie three side by side with the others curving down. That is our constellation, The Hunter. There is his hound by his side. Listen, and Nivena will sing you a tale about him and how he came to be placed among the stars."

A voice rose up in the night that made Railing tremble at first. Then the haunting beauty of the sound settled deep into his bones, drawing him deeper into rest. He listened to Nivena sing of the hunter who had mastered all manner of beasts, both natural and strange. But still the hunter did not have peace in his heart. He hunted treasures but found none that satisfied him. Finally he set out on a hunt for the heart of life itself. He chased wise men and rumor and legend all over the face of the known world. He searched the depth of the four unknown realms and even plumbed into the bowels of Hell, but he could not find the heart of life. One day he found a boatman that said he would take him far beyond the edge of the sea, to where a powerful and gifted race of men lived that had all wisdom and knowledge.

Just as Nivena sang of the hunter's journey across the sea Railing slipped away into sleep, never hearing where the song led.

When Railing awoke the sun was in the sky and a feeling of aloneness settled all around him. His couch was the only one left on the roof, and there was no sign of the Hunter King and his beautiful daughter. Peering over the edge of the roof he could see the forest had changed, as if he had slept through an entire season.

The lodge below was as empty as the roof. Dust settled all over the hallways and rustic furnishings. Cobwebs gathered in corners. The fireplace that had blazed the night before was cold and cleaned of ash. The place seemed as if it had been abandoned for many years.

Outside Railing found a horse tethered and quietly grazing. The animal had been outfitted and loaded with provisions. Hunting spears, bow and arrow, knife, biscuit, wine skins and dried meat were all packed onto the large destrier. Confusion washed over Railing. So much time had seemed to have passed yet the animal looked as if it had been prepared just that very morning.

Certain that it was all the Hunter King's doing Railing

mounted the animal which quickly eased under his hand. He looked around the clearing, up at the lodge, still sick with love for Nivena, and set out towards the river again.

Had Railing not been trained as a hunter and tracker there would be no way he could have found his way back again. But he had developed a preternatural sense of direction, and through the long hunt for the enchanted herd and the chase for the white doe, Railing had circled around closer to where all his adventures began. He knew this without knowing how or why, for that is the way that much of our giftedness works.

It wasn't long before Railing burst out of the forest and found himself standing on the road. A strange sensation buzzed in his brain, one that an earlier age would have known as home sickness. All Railing knew was that the road he stood on led back to all he had known before, and though he held no love for the things still walled up in the city, he longed for the soft and familiar places he had grown up in.

He was tempted for a moment to ride down the way that led back to the city and return home. He was certain he could manage a way over the wall now. But the love of two people made him hesitate. Alistair needed him, he needed to make amends to his only friend, and Nivena waited for him. Railing knew there was no one like either of those two in the city, and so he knew he couldn't go back. There was even a knowledge within him that was certain he could never go back even if it weren't for those he loved. Adventure had changed his life forever and some doors would forever remain locked.

As these thoughts held Railing in pause on the side of the road the sound of an approaching horse stirred him out of his reverie. Railing started and looked down the road, towards the approaching sound. And who would it be riding around the bend but Alistair, atop a shaggy mare and looking as if he too had been part of a great adventure.

Part III

By now you must know that there was another hand that guided Alistair and Railing. For what would the chances be that their adventures coincided and guided them in such a way that they would meet back on the road at the same time? Indeed, such things happen many times in our lives and we pass by them unawares, or we laugh and call them coincidence, or the luck of the draw. But in fact, these are the ways that the unseen is most visible, and the most certain assurance we have that a power much greater and wiser than us is guiding all things to a place we know not.

Neither Alistair or Railing took time to wonder at this strange work of fate. They were much too elated to see each other to care. All they could do was embrace with the special joy that comes when something dear that was lost is found again.

The men rode on and shared their stories with one another. Alistair told of his escape down the mine, his encounters with Asher and Tabitha, as well as all he had learned from the old man about Rabon and the need to rescue Bella and return her lamp.

Railing shared his story also. He nearly wept with grief as he confessed to forgetting all about Alistair's peril. Alistair for his part would admit no hurt done to him. Forgiveness came natural and without any thought, as is proper between friends.

For the first few days of their journey the two men met with no disturbances or peril. The landscape passed by them and they were able to appreciate the simple beauty of the earth. At night they stared at the fire and talked, and ate whatever game Railing had killed that day. Railing explained the flute to Alistair for he had seen them at court. Over the nights Alistair toyed with the instrument, finding a strange knack for it and producing something almost sounding like music. He also discovered the joys of sleeping under the stars and waking up with the dew and dawn.

The land slowly rose as they traveled. The terrain became rocky and soon a chain of mountains rose in the distance. There was no way to tell how long the road actually went but it looked clear that it was leading them straight into the distant peaks.

After a few days travel, when the sun began to draw down in the west, Alistair and Railing made camp beside the road not far from a tall, grassy tor. If they strained their eyes they could barely see what looked to be tall stones poking out from the top of the tor, unsophisticated and rough, but certainly the work of ancient men, though moss and vine had begun to reclaim the carved rock.

The men set camp and ate their meager rations made sweet by enjoying them in the freedom of the open road. As the fire burned down and their eyes began to droop with sleep one of them noticed a flash of light up on top of the tor.

"Did you see that?" Railing pointed up to the rocky hilltop.

The flash came again followed by a blaze of orange light. The unmistakable flicker of firelight danced on the hill. Shadows moved among the flames, figures distorted by shadow.

The sound of drums began to thump from the hill, slow at first then picking up tempo. A laugh rose up and shadows began to move among the ruins, dancing to the pounding beat of the drums.

Both men found something strangely intoxicating about the sound of the drums. At first the men didn't notice it at all when their feet tapped to the same rhythm that pulsed on the hill. Then they swayed, drawn in by the irresistible pull of the music. Then they stood and moved a bit closer, just to hear what was going on a little better.

Bit by bit they moved towards the hill, then up it. Never did they have the intent of going all the way to the top. They simply wanted to hear better this wonderful music that drew their bodies in.

As they got closer to the top the sounds of laughter echoed louder. Soon the men were scrambling over rocks, heedless of their own dash towards the drum beat. Only when they had reached the top did they pause, staring in wonder just outside the firelight at the strange scene before them.

A tall fire blazed in the circle of standing stones. Some of stones leaned forward or to the side, others had sworls carved into their face. All the stones were terribly worn and ancient, moldering away beneath the wear of countless centuries and seeming to be full of a strange and terrible power. Four men pounded four large drums with mallets that looked like bones. Around the fire men and women, all stripped to the waist wearing skirts of cloth and streaked in blue paint, danced wildly to the mad beat of the drums.

Alistair and Railing had never seen anything so strange and enticing their entire lives, but at the same time it felt familiar to them both. The beat vibrated in their bodies and they felt every joint and bone pulled as if the music had physically taken hold of them. It felt so natural to be feeling as they did that they did not think it strange to step into the firelight, right up to the circle of spinning dancers. And it felt even more natural to join the dance too, it seemed simple enough.

The men did not even take notice that they ran around the fire, whirled, then leapt into the air spinning, just as the others. A stranger would have thought them both as native as the painted men and women. Alistair could only faintly wonder at the oddity, but Railing had lost himself in it completely.

As Alistair danced he felt the story of the dancers unfolding around him. It was as if he could hear it spoken in the drums and see it danced out in the spins and leaps and the flailing of the arms. A whole history unfurled in his sight as he danced.

He saw a cold, starry night on a wind-blasted plain. A group of frightened people trembled around a small fire. They were starved and huddled together. Their sunken eyes peered fearfully out at the howling night. Rags hung off of their withered frames, and they sucked on the bones left by stronger tribes.

A split ripped open in the earth and a stranger stepped out amidst a blaze of fire. The frightened tribe cowered in the force of his presence but had not even the courage to run. The stranger danced out of the fire with a grotesque smile on his face and his body streaked in blue flame.

His name was Quotl, and his eyes bulged and his large, square teeth gleamed. A look of madness locked his face as he danced with his blue flames. Four giants rose up and pounded the earth in rhythm, causing the ground to shake with their drum beats.

Quotl taught the frightened people how to dance. As they danced the fire obeyed them. So they painted themselves with blue paint and danced around the fire.

They could feel the fire's hunger as they danced. So they cast the weak and old into the flames but the fire was still hungry. Someone cast a woman into the flames but the fire was still hungry. Then a deranged woman hurled her own young into the churning flames and the fire was pleased.

The fire exploded in a burst of heat and it gifted the people with its power. They were no longer afraid of the dark plain or the cold wind that howled or the other, stronger tribes that stole their women and their game. Now they had the favor of the fire.

The fire taught them how to dig the metals from the earth and forge them into weapons. So the tribe grew strong and feared. They preyed on the villages and the nomads and the unsuspecting wayfarer. And they never forgot to thank the fire, filling it with the bodies of those they captured.

Every new moon the tribe streaked themselves in blue paint and danced the fire. They danced as Alistair and Railing danced, as someone who knew the dance in their bones.

Alistair could still see in his mind how the tribe captured and burned their enemies alive. They danced in celebration and Alistair could feel the heat of the flames on him.

He saw them pillage a weeping town and his skin grew hot. A vision of the tribe burning a caravan came into his mind, and as they danced around the wreckage his sweat bubbled all over him.

He saw them establish a city and build a huge furnace in its center, lorded over by a sadistic priesthood. They burned their enemies and sometimes burned their children. Whatever the fire wanted they fed it. He felt hotter and hotter, as if he were a part of the fire too.

Something rose out of the heart of the furnace just as the city grew strong and wealthy. Something dark and powerful, impossible to look upon, haunted the city and consumed it from the inside out. The men of Quotl fled their city, running again onto the wind-blasted plain.

Alistair saw the land around them empty so the tribe traveled out to draw the unsuspecting into their fires. They enticed the wanderer with the sound of drums and brought him dancing around their fires, into their circle of stones, just as Alistair and Railing danced. Then he saw them....

Suddenly Alistair jarred himself awake. That final vision of unwary travelers mesmerized into the fire shot awareness into him. He looked up and found himself standing right next to the fire, the tribe dancing wildly around, pushing them closer and closer to the flames. Railing still danced, oblivious to the danger around him.

Alistair tried to grab Railing but the hunter danced on. He tried to run out of the circle but the dancers closed in and pushed him back towards the flame, their circle growing tighter and tighter, forcing him closer to the fire.

Panic surged through Alistair as he searched frantically for some aid or escape. There was nothing around to help him, only the mad tribe intent on feeding him to Quotl. He had left his light and sword and all his weapons back at the camp. He looked down and saw all that he had with him was the flute he had been playing earlier that night.

With nothing else to do Alistair put the flute to his lips and played one clear, strong note. For an instant the drummers hesitated. The dancers lost a step. They quickly recovered and danced on, pushing in tighter and tighter.

Alistair tried to play a song. He played the notes out in defiance of the drums and the dancers. But the dancers only howled and danced faster and the drummers cried out and beat the drums harder. One of the dancers shoved at Alistair and he lost the song.

The dancers circled tighter and Alistair could feel his skin burn. He closed his eyes and thought of the forest and the stars and the moon, and the lamp he carried with him, a flame that didn't burn to the touch nor could be blown out. He put the flute to his lips again and played a song that rose into his heart. He had no idea what he played, but he ignored the rising sound of the drums and the mad howls of the dancers. He let the song flow through him and he obeyed.

Instead of playing the song, the song began to play him. Alistair hardly noticed it happening. With his eyes closed he let his fingers move on their own and a song rose from the flute that made him weep. He played in his tears and the heat died away. Laughter rose up in him and he played on, filling the music with his joy.

The drummers pounded so hard their drums broke, and Quotl's music was broken too. Alistair kept playing the song of the universe, and he felt that he danced among the stars. Time slipped away from him but he played on, knowing that nothing mattered but the stars.

Then, as sudden as it had come upon him, the song ended. Alistair looked up and found that he and Railing were alone on the tor. The stone ring still surrounded them but there was no sign of the tribe or the fire or the drummers. Railing looked around confused, as if he had just been pulled awake from a powerful dream.

* * *

Over the next few days Alistair tried to play the song again. From time to time he would hear pieces in his head and he would pull the flute out and try to recreate it, but all that would come out was noise. He played other songs, and unexpectedly one would sound like that song he played on the tor. As soon as he became aware of it the song faded and he was once again playing the same regular song he had been.

After Alistair explained to Railing what had happened on the tor the two didn't talk about it again. They did become increasingly wary of anything they saw off the road. One night a child appeared near the fire and begged them to come and follow him into the darkness. Alistair held the lantern up to see and the child had disappeared.

On another occasion, when they were riding on an

overcast day, a flock of black ravens dove at them and almost struck had they not pulled up at the last minute. The flock turned and dove again. They flew around and dove, as if trying to drive the men from the road. Railing had shot three of them down before they gave up and flew off.

Both the men continued to learn as they traveled. Alistair learned the bow from Railing and continued to become more proficient with the flute. Railing studied the increasingly steep and rocky land as they were led closer and closer to the looming mountains.

One day as they approached the shadow of the mountains, just as they rose over a hill, they saw a company of soldiers lined up beside the road. Railing pulled up sharply for he noticed the banner of Lord Rabon.

"Back, back," he hissed as he pulled Alistair's mount away from the crest of the hill.

"What is it?" Alistair whispered, unaware of what the hunter had seen.

"It is Rabon's men. I don't think they saw us," Railing told him. "I even think I saw Rabon himself standing at the head of the company."

The two men slid off of their horses and crawled back up to the hilltop. Peeking over the rim they saw about twenty mounted soldiers, all bristling in arms, waiting on the side of the road.

"What do we do?" Alistair asked, feeling as if they faced their greatest obstacle yet.

"I don't know," Railing shrugged.

For nearly an hour the two men sat and thought about their predicament. Every few minutes one would crawl back to the top of the hill and peek over, only to come back with the same report as before.

"Perhaps we should just ride past him," Alistair finally suggested after they had discussed all other possibilities.

"And what's to stop him from arresting us?" Railing

pointed out. "There's no way we could fight off that many."

"The old man told me to trust the road," Alistair said, remembering Adger's parting words to him. "He said that Rabon cannot touch us if we stay on the road."

"That's good and well for talk, but now he stands there waiting for us. What's to stop him from just grabbing us?"

"I can't tell you. I just know we should trust the road."

"I don't like it," Railing insisted. "It sounds foolish to me."

"It sounds foolish to me too," Alistair agreed. "But we must do it all the same."

In a sudden burst of resolve Alistair stood up and mounted his horse. He kicked the animal into a trot and began forward quickly, lest his will fail him. He heard Railing hiss a warning from behind, then heard his friend mount and follow. Railing caught up and the two trotted down the hill together.

As soon as Rabon saw the pair the soldiers straightened up, baring their weapons of war. A wicked smile crossed the lord's face as he eyed the men.

"Halt! In the name of High Lord Rabon!" the marshal cried out to the men as they passed.

Railing and Alistair pulled up to a stop but did not leave the road. Rabon and his men made no move towards them.

"You are both under arrest for High Treason, Desertion, Escape, Violating the Lord's Peace and Traveling the Forbidden Road! Come now and beg the mercy of the High Lord! Turn away now before you forfeit your lives!"

No one moved. Rabon eyed the men with a predator's gaze. Railing and Alistair shifted uneasily in their saddles. Alistair could feel his heart pounding in his chest.

"You know I expected this of Alistair," Rabon finally said. "But you, Railing, I did not. After all the kindness I showered upon you. I trained you and sheltered you and showed you mercy and all manner of affection. And this is how you repay me."

Railing looked away from Rabon's hard stare. He opened his mouth to defend himself but found no words. He could only look away.

"Remove yourselves now from the road!" the marshal demanded.

Still no one moved.

"Remove yourselves now from the road or face greater punishment!" the marshal warned.

Neither Rabon's men or the travelers budged.

"Weapons up!" the marshal cried.

Rabon's men pulled their weapons at the ready. Their horses took a step forward, just up to the edge of the road. Alistair and Railing jumped back in alarm, their horses just staying on the path.

"Don't leave the road," Alistair warned as the soldiers moved to attack.

The weapons froze in movement. The soldiers held them up as if they were going to attack but did not throw their spears or move to slash with their swords.

"Last warning!" the marshal yelled again.

"Come on," Alistair prodded. "They can't do anything."

The two men took off slowly past Rabon and his men. The soldiers followed beside them, their weapons still at the ready.

"Last warning!" the marshal warned a second time. "This is final! We will attack!"

"You don't want this," Rabon spoke to Railing as he rode beside him, just off the road. "You loved the hunt, didn't you? This isn't your life. Why are you even on this silly quest? You know me as a good lord. I always let you have your way, didn't I? Come back, Railing. All will be forgiven. In fact, I can make you Chief Hunter. Craddock has passed his prime. You deserve that position."

"Final warning!" the marshal yelled out impotently.

"This is it! Soldiers ready!"

"Don't listen to him," Alistair told his friend. "Stay on the road."

"He doesn't understand you at all," Rabon sneered in Alistair's direction. "What does this starry-eyed poet know? You are man of action, of the world. This cry baby knows nothing but moaning and whining."

"He is my friend" Railing answered softly, still not daring to look at the High Lord.

"I am your friend," Rabon said. "He has done nothing for you but get you into trouble. I have given you your identity. I have made you a hunter."

Railing pulled up to face Rabon. For the first time he looked him in the face and challenged the High Lord stare for stare.

"He showed me danger, but he showed me freedom," Railing stated confidently. "He was my friend when there was no one else."

"Final warning!" the marshal continued to holler. "Weapons ready!"

Suddenly the marshal cried out in pain. The soldiers whipped around to see an arrow protruding from his arm. Alistair sat with his bow strung, nocking another arrow.

"You are making a mistake," Raboin warned, pointing at Railing.

Alistair fired another arrow, this time striking a soldier in the leg. He pulled another from his quiver, and before he could arm his bow the soldiers turned and scattered. Rabon alone stood beside the path, his face red with anger.

"You're next," Alistair threatened, aiming the arrow at Rabon's face.

Laughter croaked from Rabon as he stared down Alistair's arrows. With a flourish he threw his cloak off and spread his arms wide, inviting any attack with his haughty gaze.

"Those weapons cannot harm me," Rabon spat. "I am the wielder of the deep magic. I have drunk the blood of the earth and stolen the breath of the sky. The ocean depth has been my home and the mountain has yielded me its secrets. Four times I passed the fire that no fire would burn me. Three times I shed my blood on steel so no steel could cut me. I drank the water of the rock that no rock would bruise me. Seven times I burned the sacred wood that no wood could harm me. There is nothing forged or brought from the earth that can cause me any hurt or harm. What would you do to me pitiful man that you are?!!"

Rabon thrust out his hands and green fire sprang up from the ground. He spread his arms wide and laughed, the green fire blazing in his eyes.

Alistair let loose his arrow. The bolt shattered when it came near Rabon. Railing let fly his arrows also, and Alistair pelted him with as many as he could.

Rabon seemed not to notice the hail of steel that shattered around him. He sat on his saddle bathed in green fire. The arrows burst all around him in splinters of wood and shrapnel.

Finally Alistair pointed an arrow not at Rabon, but at the mount beneath him. The arrow flew and bit into the flesh of the horse's thigh.

The startled mount bucked in pain and almost threw Rabon off of his back. Green fire flickered and the High Lord fell out of his trance. The wounded mount turned and carried Rabon away over the hills.

In silence Railing and Alistair watched the High Lord carried away with his scattered soldiers. When horse and rider had disappeared they were alone again on the road. If not for their trembling limbs and nearly empty quivers they could almost believe that the confrontation never happened. It was a quality they found true of the road. Once on the road, everything else seemed not quite as real.

* * *

Four days after their confrontation with Rabon, the two men came upon what appeared to be the end of the road. The path squeezed close between two rocks on a rise in the mountains, and then abruptly ended. A valley of short grass spread below them with only a faint trace of line that wound down it, perhaps a barely discernible path.

"Is this it?" Railing asked, somewhat startled.

Two days ago they had entered the mountains. Their pace had slowed considerably as they wound through high, rocky paths. Sometimes the road even had them pressed tightly to the side of the mountain as a perilous drop fell away on the other. Thankfully, they had been harassed by no other danger since confronting Rabon.

"It seems so," Alistair noticed, disappointed in the end. "But I don't see anything here at all."

"What is that?" Railing pointed out, gesturing at a structure that lay just beyond the end of the road, partially hidden behind a boulder.

The men rode cautiously closer, wary since their adventures. The structure seemed modest enough, built of timbers and stone, with a second story rising up in the back. Smoke drifted out of a chimney but no other signs of habitation were visible.

Alistair pushed on the door and it gave way without resistance. With no other options the two men stepped inside and found themselves in the common room of an inn, empty except for a bartender sitting behind the bar cleaning a glass.

"Welcome travelers," the bartender greeted. "What can I get for you?"

Neither Alistair or Railing moved. They both suddenly felt a desire to be on the safety of the road, not trusting anything that dwelt apart from it.

"No need to fear," the bartender tried to assure them. "I am one of the original denizens of the road. You may even say I am The origina l denizen of the road. No harm will come to you here. Come, sit down."

Reluctantly, the men obeyed, taking a seat by the roaring fire. The bartender came around and brought them two mugs of beer. Apprehension still had the men frozen, not willing to trust the drinks in front of them.

"You are safe here," the bartender tried to comfort them. "No doubt you have confronted many dangers on your travels. And you must be cautious now. You would not have made it so far without a little wisdom. But I assure you that I may be trusted. You are safe here."

"A wise man told me not to leave the road," Alistair said, slowly warming to the bartender.

"And that was good advice," the bartender agreed. "Yet you have left the road, haven't you? You succumbed to the spell of the Molians. You almost burned for it.

"How did you know that?" Alistair asked in amazement.

"I told you, I am a natural denizen of the road," the bartender explained. "You may even say its my domain."

"Who are you?"

"My name is Pyrphoros," the bartender introduced with a bow. "And I am here to assist you both. Please, drink. It will ease the burdens of the road."

Railing was the first to lift his glass. He drank without hesitation and smiled as warmth suffused through his weary bones. Exhaustion peeled off of him leaving a vigor that he had not felt in days.

Seeing the content on his companion's face Alistair lifted his glass with more hesitation. One sip took all of his wariness away. He too drank deeply and felt comforted by the beer.

"Now, how about some food," Pyrphoros offered.

Without any reluctance the two men eagerly devoured the food Pyrphoros brought. The bread was still steaming and warm and sent a thrill of giddiness through them. The meat was succulent and moist and made their muscles feel stronger and more robust. Boiled greens sharpened their senses so that the light seemed suddenly brighter and the crackling of the fire popped in their ears.

"And now some mead," the bartender said as he poured two glasses of golden liquid.

The mead went down their throats smoothly, filled with sweet, heathery tastes. Contentment flowed through them as they drank. Sitting there both of the men wished nothing more than to stay in that place forever.

"Drink and rest," Pyrphoros told them. "You must resume your journeys yet."

"But where will we go?" Alistair asked. "This is the end of the road."

"This is not the end," they were told. "This is merely the end of the marked path. From here you must seek out the path without it carved beneath your feet."

"But how can we know where the road is when we cannot see it?" Railing asked.

"Are you not a tracker?" the bartender asked back. "Do you not see a path of the animal without it being marked?"

"But it is marked by the beasts passage," Railing argued.

"At the end of the day you must trust what you know," Pyrphoros told them. "The path is there though you may only discern a few feet of it at a time. And the peril is greater too. But you must believe and continue forward despite what dangers you may encounter, or what failures you may experience. Remember that. It is no great shame to lose the road, but you must always seek it again."

"I was told there was a great weapon at the end of the road," Alistair inquired. "One that would defeat Lord Rabon and his hosts."

"Great weapon indeed," Pyrphoros laughed. "Though some may not call it that. Long ago there were many pilgrims on this road, and none came seeking a weapon. But for many, many years I have been alone and waiting. No man has walked this road for a long time. And now you come seeking a weapon. It is a sign of these times that you seek for a weapon's sake. But beware you do not mistake what you find. It will most certainly not be what you expect. Rather it is exactly what you need.

"Be careful of the perils along the way. I notice you have a lamp. It is powerful and helpful but it does not belong to you. See that the one it rightfully belongs too gets it back. She needs it now more than ever."

With that Pyrphoros cleared the places and led the men back to their rooms. As Alistair climbed into a soft bed he looked out of the window beside him. A full moon rose high, shining blue light upon the mountains ahead. He could see no path, but his heart longed for him to search, to even die trying to find it.

As he looked out the window, filled with the mysterious sense of the night's beauty, he heard Pyrphoros whistling down the hallway. He recognized the song immediately. Even in the simple way that Pyrphoros whistled he could tell it was the song he had played on the tor, the one he had lost and tried so desperately to regain. He tried to get up and chase after the bartender, ask from where that wonderful song came. Something in the song held him down though. He tried to grab on to the song, to will his mind to attention. The glorious tune faded away and sleep took him.

***

When Railing and Alistair woke the next morning the inn was no more to be seen. Both men were startled to find themselves on the ground, though they bore none of the discomfort. They felt as if they had slept all night in the soft beds they had first fallen asleep in. In fact, they both felt they had experienced the best sleep of their lives. A vigor flowed through them that had each man feeling at the peak of his power.

Neither man remarked too much on the mystery of the inn. Both had become accustomed to strange happenings in the world outside the steel walls of the city. They gathered their few belongings together and prepared to leave.

For a long time the men stood at the end of the marked path and looked down at the grassy valley below. Neither had the slightest inclination as to where to go. Railing stared hard at the grass, not able to distinguish even the slightest hint of a trail. All of his hunter's training was worthless. He could not even discern a trace of a trail.

It was Alistair who actually saw the road first. He had decided to set off straight, hoping that it was right. Being stirred by a sudden conviction that they couldn't stand there forever he nudged his horse in the direction he thought best, feeling in his heart that the road knew best.

Just as he set out, just as his horse finished one step, something materialized before his eyes. A vague passage in the grass, a parting of the thin green blades was seen. It was almost too subtle to be noticed, and it only stretched a few feet forward.

"Look there," Alistair said, pointing to the newly defined path.

As soon as Alistair pointed it out Railing saw the path also. His hunter's eye discerned it more clearly, and felt more confident in its certainty. It was one of those revelations, that once seen, was difficult to understand why it had not been obvious before.

All day the men followed the path through the valley. It wound through the rim of the vale and into another, this one darkly forested. Once inside the shadow of the trees the path became harder to see, but faithfully the pair waried on.

After dark fell and camp had been set Alistair carried the lamp to see if he could make out the path at night. To his surprise he noticed he could see the road better at night than at day. Under the power of the lamp he saw the path not as a vague depression in the ground but as a trail marked quite clearly, like so many trails that wind through wild places.

Calling out to his friend Alistair showed Railing the mysterious power of the lamp. Both marveled at what they saw and debated the idea that they might travel at night better than at day. They had just come to this very conclusion when Railing noticed the red eyes staring at them from beyond the rim of the light.

"Alistair, be very still," he warned as he pointed out the glowing eyes beyond.

In front of them he saw six gleaming pairs stare menacingly towards them. He looked around and noticed they were surrounded. He couldn't make out the shape of the creatures at all, for he could only see their red eyes. But he could sense they were hungry and waiting, and desired them both as a glutton desires a meal that is set out before him.

For a long time the eyes watched them, unmoving. Neither Alistair or Railing dared leave the safety of the road. Both acutely felt their vulnerability, relying on the thin strip of trail to protect them from the pack of wild and evil things that stalked the night.

Railing felt the tension burst inside of him. He nocked an arrow and let fly at the closest pair of eyes. A yelp split the silence of the dark, and all at once the pack of red eyes scattered, leaving the men alone again with the night.

The men slept all night on the trail itself. Each huddled as close to the lamp and to each other as they could, laying long ways on the path. The encounter convinced them that day would be better to travel after all.

When morning came the woods had a sinister cast about them. The brief encounter with the evil that stalked in the dark tainted the place with its vileness. Before, neither man had noticed his surroundings, being intent on finding the path. But now they looked around warily and noticed how twisted the trees looked and how much sunlight the canopy filtered out and how grey it was for a forest. There was nothing happy that they could make out of their surroundings.

Discerning the path became more difficult as they traveled. More than once the men had to stop and survey their surroundings and try to discern what was the way and what was irrelevant markings in the foliage. Almost everyday they considered changing their travel to night time. But every night the pack of red-eyed animals returned, staring hungrily until Railing chased them away with his bow.

As fear and weariness wore on the men they became short with one another. On more than one occasion they would argue angrily about which direction they should go. Railing would declare that as a hunter he was more capable to make the decisions, while Alistair would claim that he was more intelligent and thus more fit.

The days wore on and the men began to believe that they would be in the dark forest forever. Despair sunk in and they talked less, even becoming suspicious and hateful towards one another. Their hearts began to grow as grey and droll as the forest around them.

On one particularly grey morning the two men could not agree on the path, and neither would relent to the opinion of the other. Railing could see that the path wound to the left, and only to the left. Alistair hotly declared that any fool could see the path branched off to the right.

They argued most of the morning, filling each other's ears with the nastiest, most hateful things they had ever uttered to one another. The only solution they could arrive at was they would go their separate ways, each man on the path he thought best.

So Alistair and Railing split up, the hunter riding to the left, confident that it would be the death of Alistair if he did not follow. And Alistair rode to the right, knowing that the fool Railing would come around soon enough and catch up. What the men should have done was wait until nightfall and allow the light of the lamp to show them the true way. Had they done that they would have seen clearly that neither of them had chosen the right way.

Instead both men rode their own ways, off the road and away from safety. Alistair had a sinking feeling in his gut when he was hardly an hour away from his friend. He knew he had made an awful mistake. Something didn't feel right on the road. He thought he could still make the path out, but then it would disappear altogether and panic would surge in him.

As dusk began to fall Alistair had lost all traces of his false path. Fear trickled down with the darkness. The woods closed in around and the tree branches grabbed at his face. He pulled the lamp close by and squinted out for any sign of the path. He could see nothing but the trackless woods around him.

When the sun had fully set the red eyes emerged from the darkness. Their sinister stares gleamed off the light. Alistair harried his tired mount to go faster and faster. The red eyes followed, even drew closer, seemingly unaffected by the power of the lamp.

The first beast to move into the light shocked Alistair with its hideousness. The creature ran on all fours and looked every bit a wolf save for its bare hide. Hairless black skin cracked with bleeding sores. A stench rose from pustules and the panting mouth full of brown teeth. A dark red tongue dangled from the animal's open maw.

The beast leapt and snapped at Alistair's leg. Frightened, he screamed and kicked his horse to run faster than it could. Another of the creatures fell in beside the first, just as hideous and awful. Two more quickly followed, closing in fast to rider and mount.

More animals began to appear, completely surrounding Alistair. They broke through into a small clearing and would have run into a rock wall had not his horse seen it first. On instinct the mare kicked her hind legs out, sending one of the beasts flying away into the darkness.

Alistair whipped the horse around, ready to face his attackers that now formed a circle around him. Finally remembering his sword, he unbared the steel blade. A burst of courage ran through him and he charged the circle of twisted creatures, hacking his way through.

The horse guided Alistair now more than he guided her. She took him around the rocky outcropping, the hounds still hot on the chase. Suddenly a path appeared winding up the steep rock. Without hesitation Alistair charged for the way, certain it was not the road he searched for but needing some sort of escape.

The horse struggled up the steep grade. Rocks and dust flew out from her feet. She was barely able to twist around the sharp turns but somehow she managed to maintain her feet as Alistair clung to the animal. When they reached the top Alistair rode on. He looked frantically around but saw no signs of their pursuers.

Alistair pulled the mount to a stop. He looked around, relieved but confused that they were alone. He noticed his surroundings for the first time. The broken remnants of an abandoned city lay scattered all around him.

Alistair dismounted to give his horse a rest and detached the lamp from its pole to carry it with him. He marveled at the broken city, which looked to have been of some size at one point. Now the edifices of marble and stone were half broken and abandoned, covered in dust and moldering from neglect.

As he searched a figure moved in the shadow just beyond his light. Alistair started and looked just in time to see a woman retreating into the dark. He hastened after her.

Winding through the city streets Alistair followed the strange woman through the abandoned city. He always stayed just far enough behind to catch glimpses of her white robes fluttering around another corner.

Only one time did he get close. He rounded a corner at a run just in time to see the woman pause and turn in his direction. Alistair almost dropped the lamp as he saw Bella staring lost and vacant back at him.

"Bella!" he cried out as she turned and ran again.

Though he tried to run Alistair's legs wouldn't move. A dream from long ago bubbled up into his mind. A sudden image of him laying with Bella on a stone altar as his breath stole from his body battered his mind with vividness. He wanted to run after her but something deep and primal kept him rooted in fear.

"You are wise not to run after her," a voice broke in from behind him.

Alistair turned around to see an old man sitting on the edge of what once was a glorious fountain. He shied away from Alistair's light, shielding his eyes with a torn, silken cloak of faded purple. Alistair let the lamp fall to his side and drew his sword, already backing away.

"You have no need to fear me today," the old man sighed, dropping the cloak from his eyes. "My power is nothing to be feared. It was broken long ago."

Taking a cautious step closer Alistair took in the looks of the old man. The robes that adorned his darkly bronzed figure had once been rich and fine, but today were frayed and torn. He rubbed a trembling hand across his bald head and looked towards Alistair, searching him with eyes that were vacant and completely white.

"Who are you?" Alistair dared to ask as he stepped closer to the old man.

"My name is Desterus," he answered. "Does that name strike fear in your heart?"

"No, I've never heard it before."

"You see," Desterus cried, covering his face again with his cloak. "I used to be feared for the powers of my dark art. And look, even my name is forgotten. I cannot even frighten a wayward stranger."

"Rabon this is all because of you!" he cried out, shaking an impotent fist in the air.

"What do you know of Rabon?" Alistair asked urgently.

"You wish to know my story then?" Desterus smiled as if he were invited to the king's table.

"Yes, tell me. What do you know of Rabon?"

"More than any other," Desterus told him. "He is my son. Though never was there more ungrateful flesh born to man than the offspring of poor Desterus' body.

"You see I was once powerful and feared. I was a magician of dark power. Here in Acera I ruled the shadows. Though no one would acknowledge my lordship they all came to me when they needed knowledge or power or something done that they had not the power to do. Make no mistake, I wore no crown but I ruled this city. Acera was mine."

Desterus sighed and looked at the ground. He kicked at a piece of crumbled stone.

"My downfall came through my love of ambition. There was a witch that lived in these woods around here. I heard that she could unlock the powerful magic of passion, so I sought her out. She was beautiful and dark, and with her I conjured magic that alone I never could have touched. For thirty nights we conjured and cast and unlocked the untouched powers of our bodies and my power was multiplied through her. She taught me the secret things of passion and pleasure and how to draw power out from them both.

"When I returned to Acera my considerable power had grown. Many virgins I seduced, filling their heads with enchantments and their mouths with wine I had mixed to arouse the passions. I grew in power but still I was not satisfied.

"One night I even conjured a succubus, and as she took the body of the girl I had prepared I threw myself into tormented love with her. The result was magnificent that night. With her I even controlled the power of the lightning and thunder. But she filled with child, and on the night she gave birth she was killed by the travails of labor. Rabon was born and I alone was left to raise our son.

"Early on I could tell that he possessed much of the power of his mother, the succubus. He saw many things that I could not behold. Demons and ghosts and other unearthly beings that I knew not of haunted his nursery and plagued him with fitful nights. He grew up in fear and darkness. So I taught him my arts, tried to give him the power to control the dark things that haunted him.

"And never did any student excel the master than Rabon did me, his own father. The dark arts came natural to him and he sought more and more to gain mastery over the darkness. One creature in particular caused him the greatest fear. A creature named Enlil always returned to torment his dreams. Enlil promised to kill him one day and devour his flesh. He hovered over him at night and filled his head with gruesome images of him being flayed and tortured and eaten alive, slowly bit by bit.

"There was nothing I could do to help him. Most of the ghosts and dark creatures I could expel or teach my son how to master. But Enlil I could not touch. He tormented Rabon with malicious cruelty. And the agony wore him down. I believe he even began to hate me because I could not protect him.

"So he sought deeper and more powerful magics. He plumbed into the arts so ancient I could not even begin to know how he found them. He touched the power that pulsed at the dawn of the world and still searched deeper and darker. One day he left and I did not see him for many years.

"When he returned I could not recognize him. He had been so vested with power and with arts I knew not of that he was no longer my son. He was a child of sorcery and power. He told me he was going to destroy the city, that it was too close to the road's end to allow it to exist.

"One night he raised up the Wisp, that figure you were chasing when you came across me. One by one it pulled the citizens of Acera to their death. Only I was spared. Rabon gave me that privilege. Though it was a curse. I watched the city die one man at a time, until there was only me, only Desterus remained in lonely misery. I was left the last citizen of Acera until one day I curled up here by the fountain and died."

"So you are a ghost?" Alistair asked, fearful again of the mournful figure.

"Not a ghost as you know it," Desterus explained. "I have not the substance to appear to real men, but you have the poison in you and so can see me."

"I have taken no poison," Alistair argued. "What do you mean?"

"You were bitten by one of the virhounds," Desterus told him. "Their venom is in your blood. It has the power to drive men mad."

Alistair looked over his body and found a small scratch on his ankle. The wound was red and swollen and already oozed a green mucus. Pain shot through his ankle as if discovery itself was enough to bring an onset of pain.

"What do I do for this?" Alistair asked, fearful of the poison's effect.

"You have already begun the madness," Desterus told him. "What you do not know is that several days have passed since being bitten and you see things that are no more and things that do not belong to your world and have never belonged to your world."

"Am I to die then?" Alistair asked.

"Your body will waste away unless you can find your way out of the madness," Desterus said. "But your time is already short."

Alistair looked around trying to discern what was real and what was the product of his madness. He lifted up the lamp only to see the abandoned city stretch out before him.

"Remember Desterus if you make it out," the old man called out to him. "Remember how fearful and powerful I once was. Make men tremble at my name again."

"How can I defeat Rabon?" Alistair turned to ask. "Is there something at the end of the road that can defeat him?"

"Rabon's power is beyond mine," Desterus shrugged. "The only thing he fears is Enlil, who promises yet to devour him. Why the creature hates him so I could never tell. I do know that Rabon returned and began his conquest because he believed that some woman had the key to his liberty. He said there was a woman he must possess, for she alone could free him from Enlil."

"What does that mean?" Alistair asked desperately as thoughts of Bella sprang into his mind. "Did he say who this woman was."

"His power is beyond mine," Desterus glumly repeated. "He only said there was a woman he had to possess to gain his freedom. He didn't say who or how she would. I fear whoever this woman is will become food for the demon. But do try to remember Desterus. Will you tell stories about my power? Will you make men fear me again?"

Alistair did not bother to answer the specter. He turned desperately and began searching through the city. Street upon street he found deserted darkness. He felt trapped, as if he were turning circles upon circles, ruin upon ruin, dust and dust through the miles of emptiness.

He finally crested a hill in the heart of the abandoned city and found Bella waiting for him. She wore a white dress that glowed dimly in the dark. Her skin was paler than he remembered, and she also seemed to have a light that glistened from her skin.

Bella did not speak. She held her fragile arms out to him and beckoned him with her soft, open lips.

Against his will Alistair took a step towards her. Something inside of him screamed out a warning, but he couldn't stop himself. Knowing he wasn't in control of himself any longer he moved into her arms.

The smell of pungent perfumes and oils mingled in Alistair's senses. He moved into her arms and opened his mouth towards hers. His will had dissolved and he no longer cared for anything or anyone save for the feel of Bella against him.

Just as his lips hovered a breath away from Bella's, Alistair heard the music.

He paused, turning his head away from her. The sound came in stronger. Bella stepped towards him and he felt her draw again.

Suddenly, he recognized the song. The song he played on the hill, the song that he tried so hard to recapture but always escaped him, played softly in the distance. It was the same song that Pyrphoros had whistled as Alistair drifted off to sleep.

Alistair backed away from the pale image of Bella. He could see what she was. She was a Wisp, an illusion of the thing that he desired, but one that would draw him to his death. His own power and freedom came back to him and he turned away from the apparition.

The music sounded louder and Alistair ran towards the sound. It was so perfect and yet so simple. How could he had ever forgotten that sound? How could he have not known how to play it? It was everywhere and in everything. He ran on, ignoring everything around him.

Blurs whirled around him. The city fell away and Alistair felt himself being hurled in the air. A thousand stars suddenly blazed in his vision. The song burst in his ears. Then light exploded into him.

* * *

Alistair started awake. A grey dawn surrounded him. Thirst racked him alongside a gnawing hunger that ate away at his stomach. He grasped at the ground and struggled to stand on weak legs. He felt a pair of strong hands push him back down.

"Easy Alistair, not so fast," he heard Railing say as he was laid back down.

"Railing?" he moaned, thrilled to hear the voice of his friend.

"You've been asleep for many days," Railing said handing him a skin of water. "Your fever just broke. Here, drink."

Alistair sipped carefully at the water and ate the small portions Railing gave him. As he laid back down Railing told him everything that transpired since they separated.

Not long after they went their own ways Railing was consumed with immediate regret. He feared traveling without the lamp and so hurried back to catch up. At first he tracked Alistair with his hunter's eye, but when dark fell he could see the lamp shining ahead.

Railing told how he saw the hairless dogs chase him through the forest. He caught up with him just as Alistair was cornered and then fought through. It was then that the virhound nipped his heel, but Alistair didn't notice at the time. Railing had followed him up the rocky path, all the while calling his name. By the time they both were at the top, in the midst of the ruined city, Alistair wouldn't respond to anything Railing said or did.

As Railing told it, Alistair had been caught in a fevered sleep for four days, refusing all food and drink. Railing watched over him, camped by a ruined fountain, desperate for the healing of his friend. Just last night the fever peaked, and when Railing finally gave up hope for Alistair's return to health, he awoke.

It took another two days for Alistair to regain enough strength to travel again. Any enmity he and Railing had created between them was completely gone. Alistair told him all that he learned from Desterus, though both wondered how true any of it could be. Still, he was desperate to be out of the haunted city, as much to be rid of the dark shadow it cast as his haste to save Bella from the certain danger she faced from Rabon.

They both vowed to no longer trust their own eyes to find the road. Only the light from the lamp could illumine the true path, so no matter how frightening it was to travel the forest at night, it was what they must do. They left the ruined city behind and plunged back into the forest. Railing was able to guide them back to the place they had diverged. There they waited for dusk.

When darkness had come over them the light from the lamp showed the true path. Neither to the right or the left did the sliver of road wind, but straight ahead. Though they could see only a few feet in front of them they moved forward, trusting in the power of the light.

All night long they were followed by the red eyes of the virhounds. Though the beasts growled and threatened, and even charged towards them, the men were untouched. The road protected them far beyond what they could do for themselves.

This is the way they continued on. During the day they slept and ate. At night they used the power of the lamp to show them the path through the night. Eventually they came out of the dark forest and the virhounds stayed behind.

The path rose up into the rocky mountains and sometimes thinned so much that they could hardly keep their feet on it. Sometimes it took them to the edge of the cliff. They walked atop an unknown height, battered by cold winds, and though they could only see a few feet in front and had to press themselves and their horse against the mountainside, they trusted the lamp and where it led them. Only in the light of the lamp did the road emerge clearly.

As the dawn rose one morning they saw below them a place so beautiful it made them ache. A valley of forests and grassy plains laid out beneath them. They saw animals dance in and out of the trees. The smell of fruit and fragrant flowers wafted up to them, almost intoxicating in its purity and power. A stream trickled over rocks somewhere below, filling the valley with watery music.

But most of all, both Alistair and Railing could see the road clearly winding down into the valley below.

All of the weariness of travel drifted away from the men as they trotted down the valley. Such a burst of energy filled them that they even dismounted and ran on their own legs.

Giddiness washed over them as Railing ran and Alistair danced down the road. Neither man could explain the sudden swell of joy within them, but neither could they deny it. Their limbs were so light and strong, their hearts so full of joy, they couldn't resist.

Railing laughed as he ran through a cloud of butterflies. Their wings laughed with him, swirling around his head in a rainbow of colors. He felt like he had never felt before, even in childhood. But he knew also that this is what he always wanted.

Laughter took over Alistair as he danced down the road. A part of his mind told him how foolish he must look, but he even laughed at that. He didn't care that he looked foolish, that he had no idea how to dance. His bones danced without any command or discernible rhythm.

With the laughter still in them Railing and Alistair finally settled in to a giddy walk. For a moment they forgot about the horses and even forgot for a moment the dangers that hounded them along the road. How they knew this valley was safe they could not say for sure. But there was a certainty deep within both of them that no danger could ever enter the valley nor harm would come to them as long as they stayed.

By mid morning they had walked several miles but had not the slightest ache of weariness. Their bodies felt just as refreshed as when they touched the vale's grass at first dawn. Joy and lightness walked with them, alongside an indescribable sensation of hope and well being. In this way they finally reached the end of the road.

What met them at the end of the road was hardly what any of the men expected. Both had dreamed of a broad and strong castle or a grand palace or a tower that rivaled the tallest within the steel walls of the city. What met them was an old stone building, rustic and overgrown with ivy, a squat building that had the wear of centuries upon it.

Both men paused with awe in front of the ancient building. They could make out delicate carvings inscribed on the stone, pictures that had been so worn by the centuries that their intent had become impossible to decipher. A power emanated from the building, nothing obvious. It was a subtle sensation that both men palpably felt, a certainty that the venerable structure in front of them possessed a great and terrible power.

So engrossed were both the men in staring at the building that neither of them noticed the woman standing in its shadow. Railing saw her first and gave a start in surprise. Alistair quickly followed Railing's eyes to the lady who stood watching them silently.

Without thinking Alistair believed the woman to be as old as the building in front of them. Long, white hair spilled down from her head and flowed down her tall figure. She was wrapped in a white dress, flawless except for a stain down the side that looked like blood.

But the more Alistair looked at her the less certain he was of her age. As his eyes took her in he could not see the slightest blemish or wrinkle on her face. He shook his head, wondering how he could ever have thought her old. Yet at the same time he could not dispel the thought that this woman was incredibly aged.

Railing fared no better. At first glance he too thought the woman was ancient. But when he looked at her face; smooth, olive-toned, beautiful, he also thought that she was but a young girl in the prime of her beauty. All at once she had the appearance of being young, almost nubile, while also giving off the impression of long, advanced years.

"Welcome to my home, pilgrims," the woman said in a voice that sounded like morning.

She took both the men in with her eyes. Neither could move or utter a word. Her eyes, green as summer foliage, seemed to be full of secrets and power, age and beauty, innocence and maturity all at once. Never had they seen a woman so beautiful, yet their attraction to her was as a child that longs for the arms of his mother. They felt a safety in her presence, but much more. Something within her glance, her entire presence, seemed to promise a care and nurturing that would bind up all their wounds and nurse them into true and free manhood.

"My lady, you are hurt," Railing said, pointing to the

streak of blood down the side of the lady's white dress.

"The blood is not mine," the lady answered sadly. "It is an old wound anyway, a wound suffered by my lord and lover."

"And who is your lover?" Alistair asked.

"He is the master and builder of this place," the lady answered. "It is for him I wait. It is for him that I care for and nurture the pilgrims on this road. It is him I long for. He will come back and make me his bride.

"But come, we will talk more of this later. You journey is over, and yet it has not begun in truth. Come in, rest."

The lady led them inside the old house. Within, the hallway stretched back into the darkness. Pillars of fluted wood adorned the way. An aroma of must and freshly hewn wood mixed together, giving the dusty hall a feeling of age and newness all at once.

As they proceeded down the dark hallway Alistair thought he could hear music being played in the background. He strained his ears but the sound would go away. As soon as he quit trying to listen the music returned, haunting and oddly familiar, much like the lost tune he had played on the tor.

Railing couldn't take his eyes off of the statues that lined the hallway, placed in alcoves along the wall. Carved from smooth, white marble they depicted all sorts of men and women. Some were carved alone, others in groups. One statue depicted a man in the agonies of torture, yet an ecstasy blazed in his eyes, rendering the marble with a strange sort of life. Another showed a woman weeping, so well crafted Railing expected to see the shoulders tremble with sadness.

The two men followed the lady to the end of the long hall. She guided them down a broad stair into a dark room below. A large pool stretched across the otherwise featureless room. She pointed to the steps that led down into the pool.

"You must bathe," she commanded. "Step into the water until it covers you completely, then walk to the other side. Someone will meet you there."

Alistair and Railing were made to unclothe until they were both naked. All of their belongings were thrown into a pile. A dark haired servant girl came and took them all away.

"Your clothes will be burned," the lady told them. "Many of your things you will never see again. Some will be returned. Only what is useful you may keep. But come, bathe."

Railing stepped into the water first. Alistair watched him walk into the pool, become submerged, then rise from the other side. His friend quickly disappeared into the darkness beyond.

Alistair stepped in next. The water was cold at first but quickly warmed. A strange sensation came over him that the water was penetrating into his entire body. He shuddered at the feeling of water seeping into his bones, into his muscles and even into his quivering organs. The water quickly covered him and filled his brain, almost as if he had become water.

As he stepped out Alistair felt clean as he never had before. Although he couldn't identify what exactly was different with him, he knew something was different. His mind felt clearer, his body lighter, even the very depths of his heart felt as if it had been washed through completely. Most of all, he knew with certainty that there was a reason he had been made to go through all his trials, though he could not tell precisely why. He felt for a brief moment the presence of something powerful and great, though deeply compassionate, watching over him and guiding him.

A servant hurried over and covered Alistair's naked figure. He was dried with a robe and ushered through the darkness. The servant led him up a staircase and into a humble room.

On the small bed waited a set of clothes. They fit perfectly, nothing garish or strange, just the simple clothes of a simple man. Alistair dressed and made his way out into the hallway, dimly lit by sputtering torches.

At the end of the hall Alistair opened a door out to a garden, filled with all the same light and airiness of the valley around it. The scent of a hundred flowers hit him all at once, almost violent in its power. But Alistair could only smile, eternally grateful for being there.

A table had been laid out in the garden. Railing sat waiting on one of the chairs. Like Alistair, he had been dressed in simpler garb, though different from his own.

Like everything else about the building, the table and the food that waited were of the simplest sort. Fruit and cheese, bread and roasted meat, milk and water; these were what Railing and Alistair dined upon, though they could make no complaint of the quality. The food satisfied the men as nothing else they had ever eaten.

When they had eaten their fill the lady appeared again at the table.

"Come, it is time for you to do what you have come here for," the lady told them.

* * *

The men rose and followed the lady through the garden. She took them deep through a winding path, past the garden and out again through the back of the valley. When the path forked she stopped.

"Here your roads diverge," she told the men.

"Your path is here," she looked at Railing to indicate the fork to the left. "At the end you will find a clearing and a man waiting for you. Do all that he tells you."

Railing nodded and went his way down the left fork.

When he disappeared from sight the lady turned to Alistair.

"This road is for you," she told him, her hand held out to the right branch of the path. "At the end you will see a tall, rocky spire. Climb the steps carved into the side. At the top you will see a man waiting for you. Do all that he tells you. Beware though, your path is fraught with a difficulty that your friend's does not have. You will be broken in a way that he will not."

"Why do you tell me this?" Alistair felt compelled to ask. He looked down the right fork warily though he knew he wouldn't doubt to run down it.

"You must know so you can decide," the lady told him gravely. "If you choose to forgo this you can follow the left fork when Railing returns. It will be no shame on you if you decide so. But it is what lies down the right fork that you were made for, and not many are. A special destiny is yours. It comes with a special glory, but has a special burden. Make your choice."

Alistair didn't hesitate in his choosing. He nodded to the lady and began walking down the right fork. A small spasm of doubt touched him with his first step, but the second and third steps banished all thoughts of turning back.

"May the blessing go with you singer," the lady called out to him as Alistair walked down the path. "May the song fill you and may you be the voice of the divine."

Railing suffered only a short walk before his path ended in a clearing. Seated in the middle of the clearing was Pyrphoros, the innkeeper they had met along the road. A spear rested across his lap and a bow around his shoulders.

"Greetings pilgrim," Pyrphoros hailed as Railing stepped into the clearing.

"Pyrphoros, how did you get here before us?" Railing asked, bewildered at seeing the innkeeper again.

"I know more secrets of the road than you could ever

imagine," Pyrphoros laughed as he stood up. "I am glad to see you made it."

"What are we to do now?" Railing asked.

"I am going to teach you how to dance," Pyrphoros told him.

"Is that spear the weapon that can defeat Rabon?" Railing asked, looking at the spear in awe.

Pyrphoros shook his head.

"Is that bow the weapon? Can an arrow from that bow kill Rabon?"

Pyrphoros shook his head again.

"But I thought we would find a weapon that could defeat Rabon. Nothing can hurt him."

"I am going to teach you to dance," Pyrphoros told him again. "That is the greatest weapon you can wield."

"I don't understand," Railing told the innkeeper. "How can a dance be a weapon?"

"Learn this dance well and you can topple empires," Pyrphoros promised. "No more questions now. You must learn. Take off your shoes and follow me."

Railing took off his shoes and followed Pyrphoros into the forest. As soon as the shadow of trees fell over them, along with the cool of the shade, the distant sound of music played in the distance. Railing paused and listened, and distinctly he could hear the simple tune.

The music sounded as if it came from the trees themselves. Out of the swaying branches, the rustle of leaves, the wind that stirred them. Gentle, flawless music trickled out. He could even hear a low hum of rhythm out of the ground itself. Something about the music sounded familiar.

"I can see you hear the music," Pyrphoros smiled. He handed Railing the spear and slung the bow along with a quiver of arrows around him.

"Come, let us dance to it."

Pyrphoros took off at a run through the woods. Railing followed close behind, but soon found himself winded at the great pace that Pyrphoros had set out upon.

"You have to slow down," Railing called out breathlessly. "I cannot keep up."

"That's because you are running," Pyrphoros yelled back. "Let the music fill you. Don't run. Dance."

With that Pyrphoros sped off even faster. Railing let out a burst of speed and even then could hardly keep up. In no time he could run no further. Pyrphoros quickly disappeared through the trees.

Exhausted, Railing leaned against a tree. As soon as his hand touched it he heard the music play a little louder. He looked at his hand, startled.

He touched the tree again. Again the music played louder. He closed his eyes and let the sound play through him. A wind blew and carried the strange melody on the air.

"Dance!" he heard Pyrphoros yell out from some great distance. "Don't run!"

A deep breath filled his lungs and for a second Railing thought he heard the music in the air he breathed. Rather he felt it than heard it. He breathed deep again and felt the music in his lungs. Once again he gingerly touched the tree, and this time felt the music vibrate in him as surely as he heard it play around him in the forest.

Self consciously Railing looked around to make sure no one was looking. He trotted off slowly, trying to keep rhythm to the music around him. It was kind of a half-dance, half-jog, and if anyone had seen him would have thought that Railing couldn't make his mind up what he wanted to do.

As he ran this way Railing felt his weariness start to subside. He tried not to run, to keep up his awkward dance. Then a thought came into his head that it is not with his feet that he must dance, but he must dance with his heart. When dancing, the feet only obey the music that soars in the heart. Truly, the difference between a good dancer and a bad dancer is not how skilled or rhythmic the dancer may be, it is how free he allows his heart to feel the glorious song of joy that flows through the world.

A laugh burst out of Railing's mouth as his feet took off. The song of the forest echoed, pulsed, vibrated in his heart, and he did not resist its call. He ran, faster than he had ever run in his life, and yet he felt himself run faster and faster, until he matched the speed of the wind itself.

Any weariness melted off of Railings body. Instead a surge of energy filled him until it overflowed and began to touch the things around him. Trees grew greener, wilted ferns returned to life, flowers sprung up where his feet passed, all brought to life by the power that streaked from his charged body and soul.

Pyrphoros fell in beside Railing and the two ran up the mountain together. They laughed and side by side their energy intensified even more, so even the mountain grew under their combined power, if only by a breath.

The men ran until they reached the peak of the mountain. Their bodies radiated strength as they breathed deep and full. Railing's senses all sharpened and he took in the majestic sight of the land around him, laid out for him by the peak of the mountain.

"The Song of the Forest is your song," Pyrphoros smiled and told him. "And you could never be complete until you learned to hear its music and let your bones obey their tune. You are truly a Lord of the Hunt today. Do you understand now?"

Railing nodded as he looked all around him. Though he felt the boundless energy pulse through him he felt more content and at peace than he ever had in his life. All things were well, even as he knew that the world had been torn from its balance. Things were well within him and he could endure whatever fate may batter him with.

"I have found the weapon," he told Pyrphoros. "I am the weapon."

"You are indeed, hunter."

* * *

Alistair had a longer walk than Railing. After almost an hour the forest gave way to sloped, rocky ground. He trudged over the rocks and came finally to its peak. Atop the peak a rocky spire rose up so high he could not see its end hovering in the clouds. Into the edge of the spire was carved a stair that wound around its towering height.

He climbed the spire, up the winding stair until he reached what he thought must be the dome of heaven itself. At the top a landing waited, from which he could see the whole land about him. A small fire burned on the wind-swept landing. Pyrphoros sat waiting, stripped except for a cloth tied around his waist.

"How is it you are here?" Alistair asked, surprised as Railing was to see the innkeeper, though he had no way of knowing at that moment Railing ran beside the same man.

"Put this on," Pyrphoros instructed, handing Alistair a white cloth like his own.

Alistair stripped and tied the cloth around his waist. The cold wind battered him from all directions, chilling his naked skin. He could see the castle of Rabon in the distance, and further from that the hill he had been imprisoned within. He even saw the city he had grown up in and eventually escaped. Its pale, steel walls looked pitiful and weak against the forest that surrounded it.

"What do you feel when you see your home?" Pyrphoros asked him.

"I feel pity," Alistair surprised himself by answering. "There are so many trapped in there, in such a small place.

And they have no idea how grand and dangerous the world is around them. I feel like I need to show them the truth and set them free."

"And so many would hate you for that," Pyrphoros told him. "A few would love you and follow you. But beware, those who hate you would hate you unto death."

"Why would they hate me? I only offer them freedom?"

"Because there is nothing they fear more than freedom. Behind that wall nothing can happen to them, but they are safe. If they were to be free they would fall prey to all the wild forces of the world and be threatened by the thousand deaths that man can die when he steps into the world beyond. Most would rather be safe."

"I guess it would be better to leave them then," Alistair mused. "If they want security that bad then perhaps they ought to be left to their fate."

"Your love must be greater than their fear," Pyrphoros chided. "Even to save a few you would have to risk the wrath of them all.

"You will concern yourself with them another day. For now we sit. For now we listen."

Alistair sat down across from Pyrphoros with the small fire between them. The slight flicker of flame put out little heat and did nothing to alleviate the cold that battered his naked skin.

Pyrphoros handed him his flute.

"When you are ready you will play."

Alistair laid the pipe across his lap. It was comforting to have something familiar in his hands that was also good. Pyrphoros stared at him from across the wisps of smoke without saying a word. Alistair shivered in the cold wind.

"We must be quiet and listen for the music," Pyrphoros finally said. "Listen to the wind. Tell me if you can hear the Song of the Wind."

"Perhaps if I was warmer I could hear," Alistair shivered

and said. "It is hard to concentrate with the wind beating down on me."

"You must feel as well as hear," Pyrphoros instructed. "Relax and let the cold fill you, for the cold has its song too. You will never hear the song in your resistance. Nor can you force the song to appearing. You must open yourself to it, open yourself to all that moves around you. Let it sing to you. Open yourself and let it sing to you."

Alistair tried to relax but the cold still reminded him of how uncomfortable he was. For what seemed like hours the two sat in silence; Alistair trying to keep his warmth in, Pyrphoros still with a searching glare across the fire.

Finally Alistair closed his eyes and quit trying to hold his heat in. Surprisingly, his shivering stopped. Though the cold cut him deep into his bones he did not find the chill uncomfortable anymore. Instead he was simply cold. He became cold, but the cold did not harm him. Because he was cold.

Then the wind sang.

It was a low tune. Subtle delicacies of sound danced on the air. A careless tune, almost negligent, flowed on the wind and filled Alistair's hearing. He smiled, loving the softness of the sound.

"That is the Song of the Wind," Pyrphoros told him.

Alistair lifted the flute to his lips and played the song that echoed around him. He saw Pyrphoros smile, and even felt the wind was pleased to hear its own song playing. So the wind danced around Alistair as he played, obeying the song, and happy to obey because it was the wind's joy and pleasure to dance to its appointed song. It lifted up his hair playfully and twisted it in airy spirals.

"Very good," Pyrphoros complimented. "You learn quickly."

"Is that why I am here?" Alistair asked. "To learn to play with the wind?"

"You learn quickly, now you must learn deeply. That is but one song, a part of the Great Song, one small part but infinitely vast, as they all are."

"How many must I learn?"

"All and none," Pyrphoros answered cryptically. "Everything that lives and moves has a song. Even the rocks and seas and rivers. Listen, you must learn to hear them all. You must learn to be a singer. To sing of all things."

The Song of the Wind floated by and Alistair reached out to the world around him. The tune he played for the wind still echoed in his ears, but quieter, still present and filling him up.

Another sound came on the edge of the wind. Unlike the light melody of the wind, this sound was deep and powerful, almost too still to be heard. He knew it at once for the Song of the Rock. Reaching out to touch the ground he felt the song hum through him in quiet power.

Still he reached out further. Another song came into his heart. This one sounded erratic, racing and insistent, like a thousand insects buzzing at once but at the same time making a sweet sound. Alistair knew it at once as the Song of the Bee.

He reached further.

A soothing pulse of music came swaying in. It had the feel of something old and new, like a song that had been sung for a thousand years and one sung for the first time. It was the Song of the Trees.

One by one the songs came through until Alistair felt his brain would burst. The Song of the Robin, quiet and sublime. The Song of the Grasshopper, like strings played in the meadow. The Song of the Squirrel, fast and intense of tempo. The Song of the Deer, rising and bounding in undisguised joy. The Song of the Fern, deep and rich. The Song of the Forest connected to all of them yet was its own. The Song of the Wolf, like plaintive howling on a dark night pierced into his soul like a blade of ancient sadness. The Song of the Lark lulled him in mellowed contentment, while the Song of the Hawk sent chills of freedom aching through his body.

The songs didn't stop pouring in. They crashed upon his fevered brain one after another. One never stopped, but each one played atop the one before it. Each one a different song.

Alistair couldn't bear them all. He would shut them out except for their insistence on being heard. They were the songs of life beating around him and they would not be stopped. Life soared and raised itself up and so could not stop from singing. He could even hear an eagerness in their music, for they had not had a singer in many years, so they battered him with their enthusiastic sounds, unwilling to wait, thirsting to share.

An ache built up with the pressure in Alistair's head as he tried to hear all the songs. His soul thirsted to hear as much as the earth longed to play. Order almost seeped in, blended the songs, but they slipped away into their battering, not like the cacophony of randomness, but too many sounds to hear by one mind at once.

Alistair cried out in pain as agony tore his head. He fell to the ground, clutching his battered brain. But still the music came pouring in.

"Make it stop," he managed to whimper. "It's going to kill me."

"I cannot stop the music," Pyrphoros said gravely. "Nor would I dare such a thing."

"But I will die," Alistair cried. "It will kill me."

"Better one man die, better a thousand die than to stop one note of the song," Pyrphoros said, not without sympathy. "You must learn to hear without hearing, to keep all the songs on the edge of your consciousness without them overwhelming you. There are infinite songs, all springing from the well of the Infinite himself. It will always play, always change, never exhausting its great and terrible beauty. The Song will play. Learn with the Song or perish."

Alistair could do nothing but cry out. The songs continued to pound at his head, rip at his heart, rend him until he felt that every nerve was on fire and every fiber of his being was being stretched apart.

Then, it suddenly fell quiet.

All the sounds left at once, or rather faded as if on cue. Sudden relief flooded into Alistair. He looked up, saw Pyrphoros keeping watch over him. The sun was going down. It was twilight.

"You have survived the day," Pyrphoros said. "It will be easier after this. Now listen, all that is important will be sung next. This song you must not forget."

The sound of sweet longing seemed to flow out of the sun. Alistair knew it for the Sound of the Twilight. It made him sigh with longing and contentment all at once, as sunsets will do to man's heart. Then, as the sun faded, and the darkness pulled her veil over the face of the world, a more sublime song came in on its heels.

Although he could barely hear it, the Song of the Night seemed a song full of power. It radiated mystery, whispering to him in long, drowsy notes, like silk being drawn across his face. Alistair felt himself swaying unconsciously, drawn in by the irresistible sound. There was something to the music that promised pain, but a pain that would lead to glory.

"The Song of the Night is not for you to learn," Pyrphoros said, shaking him out of reverie. "Perhaps one day, though I would not wish that pain on any man. No, look up."

Alistair craned his head up and gasped. Millions upon millions of stars blazed out across the dark, spangling the heavens with showers of brilliant light.

And they all sang. They sang a glorious song that made Alistair tremble with wonder and awe. It was high and noble, yet perfect and humble, holding in it all the secrets of the world.

"The stars are the heralds of the world," Pyrphoros told him. "They tell the story of what was and is and will be. They sing the Song that all the earth dances to."

Alisatir listened to the music, and unlike all else that sings, the Song of the Stars contained words also. He listened raptly, hypnotized by their power.

> *Hear O mortals, the song of your Maker,*
> *When He sang all things into being!*
> *Hear of the heavens and the earth, springing from the will of the boundless will*
> *Before there was earth or sea, before night or day covered the sky*
> *Before the sun first kissed the world in glorious dawn*
> *There was the Song Master*
> *The Song Master stood upon the edge of the deep and opened his mouth to sing*
> *And from Him the Eternal Song sprang forth, begotten in eternity, of the same essence as the Singer Himself.*
> *And the darkness trembled and the deep shook*
> *From the Song came light, and the light filled the universe, putting the dark to rout and lifting the universe to glory*
> *From the Song the earth and heaven were sung into being:*
> *The waters above, the earth beneath and the waters within the earth, the sun and sky, moon and oceans, valleys and mountains*
> *And the Song bathed the earth with His music, and everywhere His notes touched, new life sprang forth -*
> *Fields of green, beast of wing, creatures treading on the ground, fish of water, mountain sprawling high, forest tree reaching out to touch the heavens.*
> *All creation danced, and they loved the song that had sung them into being, they danced each to the music given*

and as the music gave.
There was a rest, then the song began again.
It poured out abundance, a share of love within its own heart
And he thus crafted man, chief of all the workmanship of the song
A singer himself man was made, shaped to echo the splendor of the Eternal Song and dance as no thing made
A shaper and a singer and a song writer himself
The Amen crowned the world, and the Song Master poured his joy out on the Song.

All night long Alistair listened to the stars sing of the Eternal Song. He listened as he knew it wasn't the complete song, for there is never fullness in eternity, but it was the constant expression of the music, forever unfolding and forever new.

He listened to the stars sing of how man was made to be a singer, how at first he took his gift and made new songs. And the songs pleased the Singer, for they were variations of the Eternal Song, echoes of what forever unfolded around them.

He heard one day of a singer that rose up and played music that was not the Eternal Song. A snake had whispered in his ear that he had the power to sing his own music if he but chose to write it. For the snake had no power of music himself, and he hated the song that made him dance.

The stars moaned as they sang of man's fall. When he had sung his new song, the song of himself, the sky grew dark and a cloud passed over the heart of life. The Eternal Song grew dim, for the man loved his own music.

Weeping, the stars told how the man brought his people new music, and they loved it though it was not the Eternal Song. The song gave them power, and they wished to be their own masters, not bound by the song that flowed from

Heaven.

So the man made himself an outcast, lost to the song that made him. Some still tried to sing as they were made, but the Song grew dimmer and dimmer, until only hints remained, a few plaintive notes that flowed to good men in visions and prophecies and in the fleeting cry of dreams.

But the stars sang on. They sang of how the Song Master looked with grief at what he had made. Man, lost in discord, sang a million different songs but all the same dreary music, all the song of the darkness in his heart.

Alistair listened as the stars sang of joyous change. They sang again of the Eternal Song, who moved with love, became a man himself, both human and the fullness of the Song. He taught men how to sing again, how to hear his voice and dance as the universe bid him dance.

The darkness trembled and fled.

He heard how the singers of themselves hated the Song made flesh, for he showed their music the lie that it was. In dark plots they killed him and laid his body in the ground.

The stars trembled as they sang of how the Song could not die, and came to life again. This time it rose in a fullness that had never been heard before. The clouds over the heart of life were broken and the light that shined at the dawn of the world blazed in new splendor.

Alistair heard how the darkness still rested in man's heart. He heard how the Song fills him with the light and could fill him greater still. He heard of the triumphs of the light and the advances of the dark. How one day the dark would be vanquished, and even now the powers of the light, ignored as they were, shined brighter than anything the dark could mar with shadow.

In rapture Alistair listened. He heard even of himself and his own times. He heard how man had forgotten again and either hid himself from the glory of the Song behind walls, or chased after phantoms of the Song and served the magic of darker, malevolent things.

The stars sang to him the story of how the Song had sought even him out. They sang of the desire of the Song put on his heart, the love of the Song upon Railing's. They sang of how they guided them through all their trials and wanderings, and Alistair knew then that never had a thing happened to him that was not guided by the Song, and never could he fall beyond its power and love.

Finally, the stars sang of things to come. They sang to Alistair of the hunger of the world, how it languished in a misery it neither saw or knew. They sang to him his destiny, to be the singer all creation has waited long for, to restore the songs again to the heart of man. They warned him of trials and hatreds, and the evil that sought to undo him. But it also sang of triumph and coming glories, and it sang a faith into him to trust the Song that had not left him lost in all that he had done.

Alistair listened to the stars and loved the Song, and pledged his life to teach all men the glorious music that shook the temples of heaven.

The night waned and the song faded from the stars. A rosy light filled the eastern sky, just peaking over the rim of the horizon.

"Prepare yourself man," Pyrphoros spoke for the first time since night fell. "You have heard songs that spring from the Eternal Song, small pieces that creation sings and dances to. Now, hear the Song itself, the one born from eternity, reigning forever."

"Is it possible?" Alistair asked. "That my ears could even hear the fullness of the Song itself?"

"No ear can hear the fullness of the Song except the Singer and the Song itself," Pyrphoros told him. "What you will hear is what the Song sings today, what it cries out to this dawn as it cries out to every dawn, singing to the day what the day should be. You can hear it today, young singer, and you could hear it everyday from here to eternity and never know the fullness of the Song that sings eternity into being.

"Silence now, and listen to your master sing."

There was a quiet over the whole sky above him and the plains beneath. But it was not the silence of no sound. It was the silence of anticipation. Even the stars seemed to hold their breath in eagerness of what might come.

Alistair stood up and looked to the east and thought he heard a quiet, single strain of music peak tentatively over the horizon. It was almost a shy sound, as if it knew what an unworthy herald it was. Then, total silence dropped over the world, a swell in the earth and sky, then...

The dawn rose and a single flash spilled over the horizon and filled the plain with light.

All at once a song burst out that shook the whole world and made Alistair tremble with fear and joy. The forest joined in, the sky joined in, the ground and the beasts and the mountains and even the insects lifted their voices to the Song of the Dawn that was the Eternal Song itself bringing all the world to life again.

A force jolted through his body and shook Alistair to his knees. Pure joy coursed through him, almost burned him with intensity as the light spilled over him and sang the most glorious, simplest, most profound music he had ever heard. Every fiber of his being, every cell in his body quivered and shook, and it felt as if he were on the verge of exploding.

Alistair opened his mouth and laughter roared out of him. The sound that came from him was like nothing he had sounded before. The joy that tore through him paled all human laughter and washed over him in a tidal wave of ecstasy. Tears poured from his eyes, streamed down his face in endless pools and rivers, rolled down his body and soaked the cloth tied around his waist. All at once he laughed and wept for no other expression of the human body could contain the power that flowed through him, lifted up by the ineffable music that flashed and cried out in the dawn.

Dizziness took over Alistair as the feelings became unbearable. He cried out in pain and joy, the sound torn from his mouth and screamed over the plain, then he fell to the ground unconscious.

* * *

When Alistair awoke he was alone on top of the spire. The day had progressed to late afternoon, though in honesty he could not be sure he hadn't slept for days. He reached a hand out to the ashes of Pyrphoros' fire and felt no heat. He must have slept for days.

The joy of the dawn still tickled his body. The mere memory was enough to make his belly quiver. So much power and joy had been in the light, in the music.

Remembering the songs he paused and reached out to the world. Just as before he could hear the music the world sang. All around him the different hills and trees, birds and beasts, insect and field all sang their appointed song. He couldn't help but laugh as he heard that blessed music.

Alistair looked around the plain again, focused his eyes on Rabon's castle standing small in the distance. He turned and made his way down the steps of the spire, twisting down and around until he reached flat earth again.

Railing was waiting for Alistair when he returned. A bow and a quiver of arrows hung over his shoulders. In his hand was a spear that he had not seen before. The hunter smiled big and wrapped Alistair in a tight embrace.

"You're back, thank goodness," he said with a grin. "I didn't think you'd ever make it back."

"How long have I been gone?" Alistair asked, not sure if he wanted to know.

"Three days," Railing told him. "The lady told me you

were sleeping most of the time, but I couldn't wait to have you back."

As if on cue the lady appeared, still emanating that strange sense of youth and incredible age. Alistair looked at her with a deep sense of love, marveling at her beauty, though his love and admiration was exactly the same a child has for his mother.

"You have returned singer," she said to him, her voice carrying its own secret of music. "I am glad to see your trials are over. Now your true journey begins. Come, the time is upon us."

They followed the lady back into the ancient building. Down they went through a dark hallway until they arrived at a vast room lined with tall, fluted pillars. Sunlight spilled in through windows that covered the walls on both sides. An altar waited at the far end of the room upon which sat a goblet and a plate of bread. Beside the goblet waited Bella's lantern, still burning clear and bright.

"Kneel," the lady instructed them as they approached the altar.

Both men obeyed and knelt reverently before the lady in the white gown. Alistair noticed the blood stain still stood out on her otherwise unblemished dress.

"Take, eat," she instructed as she placed a piece of the bread in their mouths. "Let this nourish and strengthen you for your travels ahead."

"Drink this," she said lifting the goblet to their lips. Alistair could taste the rich wine deep in his heart. He even thought he heard a song come from the crimson wine.

"Let this cleanse you and fill you. By drinking you have sealed our covenant. You belong to me now. You serve the Song until he comes to claim you whole."

Both men uttered their agreement and knew that everything the lady said was true. They both belonged to the Song, and their lives were forever dedicated to what must be done.

"Here, take these for you journey," the lady said holding two necklaces up, each with a large, round charm at the end. From inside the charm glowed a small, but powerful light.

The lady held the charm up for the men to see. The round ball was made of silver, covered in decorative screen work. Through the elaborate screen Alistair could easily make out the pure light beneath. The lady showed them how to open the ball and inside glowed a small candle. She slipped the necklaces over their heads.

"Like the lantern that was borrowed this light can never go out, nor will it ever fail. Unlike the lantern this light belongs to you, so in many ways is much more powerful than a borrowed light. Always walk in its power and always trust in the way that it guides you. The path ahead is long and difficult and fraught with many troubles. Stay always in the light and you will prevail.

"Now the time is upon you to leave. You must return this lantern to the owner, for even now her life hangs in peril. She needs it like she has never needed it before. The world needs its song returned to it. Go, may the Song guide you and may you always rest under its shelter."

A door on the other side of the altar opened up and outside Alistair could see their horses grazing lazily in the valley. The men got up to leave. Each one knelt again before the lady and kissed her hand.

"May the Song bless you hunter," she said to Railing as she placed her hand on him in benediction. "Remember the Song of the Forest, especially its incarnation in you, the true Song of Railing. May the forest always shelter you and bring you nourishment."

"Have strength singer," the lady told Alistair as he knelt. "Never forget the Song. Though men will hate you for it you must not only sing of the Eternal Song, but show men how the song flows through them. Every creature has a piece of the Song given to them. They need a singer to draw it out of them. Remember, that is the task given you and you will fail in nothing."

Alistair kissed her hand and rose to leave. She gave him Bella's lantern and urged he return it with all haste. Outside the valley still flowed with light and power. He found his clothes folded on the horse and after dressing again they mounted their waiting horses and reluctantly left the valley.

They rode slowly as they climbed the hill out. At the crest they looked back again, drinking in one more sight of the deeply vibrant colors below them. On the other side the world seemed drab and grey, like it didn't possess the full strength of color that the valley contained.

"Maybe one day we can come back," Alistair said, voicing the reluctance in both of their hearts. "Let's go now."

Once outside the valley the men hurried on. Though they passed through the same lands as before they did not feel the same sense of danger as before. For one, the path before them was clear. Though not large and wide it was still unmistakably defined. Neither of the men could figure out why it had been so difficult to see on the way in.

That night in the dark woods the red-eyed creatures gathered around again. Being on the road and now protected by three lights the men were hardly threatened by the creatures. Still, Alistair rose and took out his flute, searching the dark for the right song.

He felt corruption of the Song for the first time and his heart faltered. All around the woods he felt the sickness, the wrongness that made him swim with nausea. He gagged and fell to his knees as a cold sweat washed over him in shudders. How can I sing in this, he asked himself. A feeling of despair over his task took over him for the first time and he hadn't the slightest faith that he could overcome it.

In agony he gripped his chest and felt the candle hanging

around his neck. He pulled it out and opened it, his eyes cleansed by the light. Immediately new hope filled him and deep within came the assurance that no matter how corrupted, how twisted and perverted the Song may have become, it was stronger still than any evil that had distorted it.

Alistair reached out again, deep into the forest. He reached back beneath the corruption and beneath the haze of sickness. He pushed back his own nausea and revulsion, his shuddering at the wrongness, and reached to hear not only the Song of the Forest, but the song of this particular forest, a piece of the Eternal Song that still flowed in it.

Finally he touched it and placed the flute to his lips. Alistair played the song that the forest should have heard but failed to dance to. Years of corruption had twisted the song and the dark woods fell to death and decay, even twisting the animals that lived within.

As soon as the notes of the song left the flute, the virhounds howled in agony. The red light in their eyes flickered and they rolled around in agony. Alistair kept playing and some of the hounds died, the red glowing in their eyes fading while some ran off, never to return to harass the men.

During the days as they traveled through the dark woods Alistair played the true song of that place whenever he could. Around the path the grass grew greener and the trees seemed stronger and not nearly as ominous as they had before. Deep in the woods they could see that corruption still kept its deathly grip, but around Alistair the song was able to restore some life.

They made haste on the journey back. Alistair played every night of the songs he heard around him. Railing grew in strength and in faith in the Song, and he loved to hear it every night. Both men spoke of their experience with Pyrphoros, sharing what they had learned of their destiny.

Alistair would play the Song of the Forest for Railing and the hunter's heart would soar.

It was odd to look at the road on the return journey. Much of what had brought them terror hardly failed to stir their hearts. When they reached the pass, the place where the path turned back into a broad road, a sense of how far they had come struck them with particular power. They thought of who they were when they left the city, scared and ignorant and seeking what they knew not. Now they were changed men, and though they knew the road before them it was still a road of uncertainty, a road that led to places they knew not.

But they trusted the road. And they trusted the Song that led them. Perhaps that is what made all the difference. For though wildness and uncertainty still lay ahead, they trusted the forces that guided them, and though the wildness could not be controlled, it promised to give all the fullness of blessing that a safe and predictable life can never come close to offering.

They traveled quickly, and in much less time than it took to arrive they had made it back to the realm of Rabon's power. An uneasiness had been growing in both Alistair and Railing as they drew near to where their adventures had begun. Though their faith was strong it was encountering its first real test, and both men wondered if what they possessed really could stand up to Rabon's power. It was not magic and steel like his, after all. How could their feeble power, they both thought to themselves, really stand up to Rabon. Neither man expressed his doubt and so it festered in them into fear.

As they came near to Rabon's castle the men decided to first pay a visit to the old man Adger. As best as Alistair's memory could serve they were able to find the cottage. Adger was overjoyed to see them.

The old man convinced them to stay with him overnight before riding to confront Rabon. They told him of all their adventures over a hot soup and fire. Adger delighted in every word they uttered. He was most especially glad to hear of Alistair and the Song.

"Do you think you might play it for me," Adger asked, hesitantly, almost shyly, on the verge of tears.

Alistair gladly acquiesced. Taking out his flute he closed his eyes and thought back to the stars, to the irresistible flow of music that echoed from them. He let the music flow through him and played pieces of the Eternal Song as it was sung by the heavens.

Adger wept as he heard. He wept and dropped his head into his hands, shuddering with the tears that overcame him. When he looked up finally a smile was spread across his face and it looked as if thirty years had dropped from him in an instant.

"I thought I would never hear that song again," the old man said. "Many years ago I heard it and it has delighted my heart to even remember it. But to hear it? Oh what ecstasy."

The old man stood up and laughed. Alistair continued the song as Adger danced around the room, as careless as a boy playing alone in the forest.

When he was finished an idea came to Alistair.

"I have a special song for you," he told him.

Reaching out around the room, among the tools and the scraps of silver and the implements of his trade, Alistair sought the notes he needed. Since Adger was loyal to the Song and had danced in obedience, the sound flowed through the room in truth and clarity.

Putting the flute to his lips again Alistair began to play the Song of the Silversmith. Another smile broke across Adger's face. He giggled and looked to his tools. Immediately he set to work, drawn by the song and his own loving obedience. Long after Alistair had stopped playing, and he and Railing had fallen exhausted into sleep, they could hear the ting of tools on silver.

* * *

The next morning as the men stood to leave, Adger hugged them both and wished them well on the peril that lay ahead.

"Thank you for that song," Adger thanked him through newly forming tears. "For both of them. Actually, they inspired me. I have begun to make a special gift for you. I'll give it to you when it's done. Be careful boys, and may the Song go with you."

After making their farewells the men set off again, this time without delay to the castle. Alistair played as they rode. He played the Eternal Song, or what he knew of it, in order to set their hearts to courage. Even then their private fears began to take over their souls, and with fear came doubt. By the time they reached the castle each man quietly feared there was no hope to their quest at all.

The village surrounding the castle was quiet and deserted as the men rode through. They could feel eyes on them though, expectant and fearful. A few times they saw a figure darting behind a corner or a curtain fluttering closed. Their fear grew but they rode on. Alistair, on an unspoken instinct pulled the hood closed on Bella's lantern so no light was seen coming from it. Both their own lights they wore proudly over their shirts.

As they rode into the castle courtyard a set of guards came out, numbering nearly twenty. They surrounded the men on either side.

"You are both, hereby arrested in the name of his High Lordship, Rabon, ruler of all the realms," the chief guard said as he took hold of Railing's stirrups.

The guards took Railing's spear and bow, but made no search of the men. They were roughly ushered into the castle and taken to Rabon's court and pushed before his throne.

As before, the court was filled with the effeminate and perfumed courtiers that hovered around the throne. Ugly and heavily painted women fanned their faces next to pale men who held dainty kerchiefs up to thin noses. The place reeked of foul human odor covered with cheap ointments and oils.

Rabon sat rigid on his throne. He attempted an arrogant smile but Alistair and Railing could both see fear in his eyes. Their confidence grew but a hair, though all they were aware of was their growing fear.

Behind Rabon's throne Alistair saw Bella and his heart nearly stopped.

He could hardly recognize the girl, so completely had she been changed. He could still see the beauty she possessed, for that had hardly been diminished. But it was marred. Her face had grown pale and thin, and her limbs hung in lifeless apathy.

Even more miserable than this were her eyes. Whereas before they shone with a secret sadness and undeterred hope, they now stared out lifeless and uncaring around her. It was as if the life had been taken from her and all that was left was a corpse being dangled by an unseen puppet master.

"You have met my fiancé, have you not?" Rabon said with a genuine and arrogant smile as he saw Alistair's face drop upon seeing her.

Bella nodded mechanically towards Alistair, although a flicker of recognition passed through her. For a moment her former self almost broke through. The mask quickly fell back down and the light fled.

"We are to be married tomorrow night," Rabon told him. "Though you will not be around to see it I fear. No, a special punishment I will mete out for both of you. For no greater enemy of the kingdom has there ever been. Not only do you defy me, spurn my kindness, and travel along the forbidden road, you now have the arrogance to come back into my presence."

Alistair could think of no response. He looked to Railing who seemed equally at a loss. For the moment he only wished to return Bella to her form.

"Have you nothing to say for yourselves!?" Rabon spat.

His sudden burst of anger made the room jump. Alistair and Railing felt their own hearts jump.

"Well? What have you to say of your defiance?"

"Perhaps you would allow a gift for the upcoming bride," Alistair offered. "A token for her future happiness."

Rabon laughed, delighted at what he believed was Alistair's attempt at humility.

"You wish to bring me gifts now?" Rabon laughed. "After you defy me and are returned to my power you want to give me gifts? What a farce. But give, please, what do you have to pacify me?"

It is most certainly true that Rabon should have been suspicious of anything that Alistair would deign to give to Bella. And for sure a flicker of suspicion passed through him. But Rabon was arrogant. And at first he feared Alistair and Railing's return, uncertain of what they might have found. For he knew that there was indeed something at the end of the Forbidden Road that could kill him.

But as he looked at the men now, trembling and fearful, their eyes cast to the floor, he knew there was nothing for him to fear. He knew for certain these men had no great weapon, or any weapon great enough to kill him. Had he not been the one to plumb the depths of all the world's magics? Who could kill him? It was really a ridiculous notion after all.

Besides this, Rabon could not pass up the opportunity to torment Alistair. He hated him with a hatred he could not explain. Never had he encountered a man he wanted to humiliate and break like he wanted to break Alistair. And if

Alistair thought he could buy Rabon's favor, then the lord would delight to give him a brief hope before tearing it away.

"Come then, give," he told Alistair. "Perhaps I will give you a reprieve if your gift delights my bride."

Rabon waved Bella forward to receive her gift. He watched with wicked delight as the girl stepped obediently forward to receive. As she stood in front of Alistair he stared into her eyes, searching for a flicker of her former self.

It flashed briefly again, but it was there. It was like a curtain being pulled aside, just for an instant, and a timid watcher stealing a glance from behind. Alistair could see she was still there, still the hopeful, dreaming, beautiful woman he loved.

"I have only this humble lantern to give you," Alistair said, pulling out the lantern that Bella had given him and had guided him when all else was lost.

Rabon saw the danger too late. He leaned forward to stop Alistair but was far too late.

Alistair threw back the hood of the lantern and the unquenchable light fell upon Bella's face. Immediately, she was transformed. The light entered her eyes, lit up her face, filled her body, mind and soul with its magical light.

A murmur passed through the room as Bella took hold of the lantern and held it up. Rabon screamed and covered his eyes.

"Take that from her!" he screamed out to his guards.

The Captain stepped forward to grab the lantern but found he could not touch it. As he reached forward his hands burned so great that he had to pull them away. Other guards tried to the same result. No matter how they tried to cover their hands no one could touch the lantern as long as they tried to take it by force.

Bella looked at Alistair breathlessly. She threw her arms around him and wept into his shoulder. Just as Alistair returned the embrace she was roughly torn from him.

"I may not be able to take the lantern but I can take her," Rabon said holding Bella roughly by the hair. "And I can take you too. Guards!"

Before the guards could come near Alistair placed the flute to his lips. He played the Song of the Stars, the very same they had sung to him. The guards paused and silence dropped over the room. Never had any ear heard the sound that flowed from Alistair and the flute. Even Bella paused, never knowing that sound could be so beautiful. For a second Alistair had the room in his hand, enchanting them, filling their hearts with dreams, unlocking the cage of the many captive souls and setting them free to soar into a sky they never knew was even there.

Abruptly the sound died as Rabon snatched the flute from Alistair's hand. He flung the instrument to the ground and it shattered into pieces. Alistair felt all his hopes break with it, shattering in his heart.

"Enough with this foolishness!" Rabon screamed. "Take them away!"

Whatever spell Alistair had cast over the room had been broken. The veil, that for a moment the song lifted, fell quickly down again, casting the pale shadow of despair and emptiness over their eyes. Only Bella remained moved.

As the guards took hold roughly of the men Alistair looked back at Bella. She stared at him with unexpressable sorrow as he was dragged away, clutching the lantern to her, tears streaming down her face, but wholly returned to life by the power of the light.

Alistair and Railing were manhandled down into the depths of the castle. There they were thrown into a dark cell, meant to be left in total darkness. Yet the lights that hung around them still shined, even brighter in spite of the dark around them. The guards made no attempt to take the lights. They slammed the rusted doors shut and locked them in fast.

Things had happened so fast Alistair barely recognized

what was occurring. Finally alone with Railing in the dark cell, he felt the weight of his failure. Not only that, but the sense of emptiness with his flute shattered, the only weapon he truly had, now gone, made his heart sink beneath a weariness he had never felt before.

"Well, we've been through worse I gather," Railing tried to encourage cheerfully.

"We have nothing though," Alistair pointed out.

"We had nothing before."

"Yes, and the result is still the same," Alistair despaired, throwing himself onto the stone floor. "Whether we were helpless or not we end up the same. We had the only things the Road could give us and we still failed miserably. Rabon disarmed us without effort. What is the point in resisting?"

* * *

For three days Alistair and Railing sat in despair in their dark cell. They ate the stale heels of bread and weak broth thrust through the door. Hardly a word passed between them. Alistair stared up at the dark, feeling the misery of his failure pummel him with regret. Railing would try to rally his spirits now and again, only to be met with empty sighs from his friend.

Through those days Railing was able to keep his own spirits up by remembering the Song of the Forest. Unlike Alistair, he knew only one song, but in the dungeon it was able to fuel his spirits more than the many that echoed in Alistair's heart. But the dark, despairing days began to quiet the music in Railing too. Hopelessness crept into his heart also until the Song was only a whisper inside him, the memory of running free through the trees dim and distant.

"Can you play a song for me?" Railing asked one day as he feared he would forget altogether.

"I can't play," Alistair said. "My instrument is

destroyed."

"Can you sing it?" Railing asked. "Or even hum it. I'm afraid I will forget it. I need to hear the Song of the Forest again."

"I can't hear it here," Alistair said. "I can hear no song but the Song of Dread and Doom."

Railing nodded and turned away from his friend. Alistair could see his shoulders shaking and heard the quiet, but distinct sounds of weeping. His heart broke for his friend whom he did not ever remember seeing cry. The sympathy he felt for Railing for a moment cracked the selfish agony he wallowed in. Misery is only a mirror where we gaze in sorrow at ourselves, and so cannot see hope because we stare only into our own clouded eyes.

As he heard Railing weep Alistair was able to forget his own pain for a moment. He wanted desperately to help his friend but could not hear the Song of the Forest. As if remembering it for the first time, Alistair pulled out the light that hung around his neck. He looked deep into its magical flame, and as it pierced his eyes that awful weight of despair began to seep out of him. For the first time since he was thrown into the dungeon he began to see, and the solution to their problem made itself appear to him. In fact, it was so simple a solution that Alistair felt a fool for not seeing it before.

True, he may not be able to hear the Song of the Forest. Instead, he looked inside Railing, past all the hurt and disappointment, the twistedness that the world had imposed upon his soul; deep within this he was able to hear a song. It was not the Song of the Forest, but it was like it. It was the Song of Railing. Not a Song of the S elf, a song made by man to glorify himself. It was a song that was put into Railing by the Eternal Song. It was the song of who Railing was meant to be.

Alistair closed his eyes and began to hum. He let the

music fill him and let himself rise and fall with the ranging notes. It was a quiet song he hummed, full of strange power and vibrating with life. He felt stronger in the song and hummed louder.

When Railing heard the music his heart lightened instantly. He recognized the song though he had never heard it. He swayed and hummed along with Alistair, reveling in the way the music brought light into his soul.

As soon as Railing joined in Alistair felt the power of the song grow. Words began to fly into his mind, words he did not understand but went with the music. So Alistair sang the words, and the power of the song grew even more.

Suddenly Alistair remembered all the songs he had learned, and they had words to them too. He laughed as a truth dawned on him, and with that realization all fear left him. Railing looked queerly at him.

"I've just realized something I should have known all along," Alistair told him. "I have been thinking that I am the singer and the flute was my instrument. And while that is partly true that isn't the real truth. The real truth is that I am the instrument, and the singer is much greater than me, for he sings all things into existence and he sings them into all their days and hours. Rabon cannot take the song from me anymore than he can take the scent from a flower."

As the song returned to Alistair he couldn't help but sing. Out of gratitude at the song's return and at joy in the song itself he sang.

With the return of song the dungeon brightened considerably. Even though it was the same cold, dark and miserable place, the music somehow transformed it. It didn't seem to possess the same dreariness as before. Nothing had changed about the place, simply the presence of music transformed the men so that they could see their prison in a new light.

So what that it was made of grey rock. Was rock not of

the earth as were the trees? So what that it was dark and cold. Does the darkness not have its own beauty? Does the cold not also have a purpose? Is the winter not as crucial as summer in the cycle of living things?

All sorts of songs came streaming back into Alistair's heart. Some he had heard before: the Song of the Wind, the Song of the Trees and Flowers. Some he heard there for the first time: the Song of the Cave, the Song of the Earth's Water. Even some he had no idea where they came from.

Most of the time he hummed the tunes. Other times words came to him as well as music. Sometimes the words were in his own tongue. At other times he didn't understand the words that flowed from his mouth. Yet they were all part of the Great Song, so he sang them faithfully as he could, never straining or forcing the songs, only letting the music rise in him and flow out unfettered.

Other prisoners gathered by the bars of their doors to hear Alistair sing. They wept and laughed and asked him to sing ones they came to love. Before long the mood over the whole dungeon brightened. Even in prison those captives tasted a freedom they had never known before.

It wasn't long before the guards too were moved by Alistair's music. They softened first towards him, then towards the other prisoners. Kindness took over where before there was only cruelty. And even though Alistair and Railing both longed for release, they found life bearable in their dungeon.

Eventually Alistair was able to hear into the guards and sing the songs that were meant for their lives. To more than one he sang the Song of Planting and Sowing, to another the Song of the Soldier, and to another the Song of the Fisherman.

One day, after the men had been locked up for nearly a month, a pair of visitors were allowed into the cell. They came in darkness, ushered in by a nervous looking guard.

"You have ten minutes," the guard whispered.

The men removed their hoods and smiled at Alistair and Railing. The two prisoners returned the smile, for they immediately recognized one of the men as their friend Adger. The middle aged man with him, with the balding wisps of hair, the pointed nose and stooped back they did not know.

"Adger! How did you get down here?!" Alistair exclaimed, embracing the older man heartily. "How did you convince the guards to let you in?"

"I am a silversmith," Adger winked. "And silver can get you anywhere. Besides, the guards seem to favor you. It didn't cost me near what I would have paid.

"But here, our time is short. Our reunion must be quick. This is my friend, Reynault. He wanted to meet you."

Alistair and Railing greeted Reynault cordially.

"He makes musical instruments," Adger explained. "Very talented. He helped me make this."

Adger reached into his cloak and presented Alistair with a silver flute. The instrument shined brilliantly in the light of the small candles. Etchings and filigree vined along the instrument, adding even more to its beauty. Alistair stood speechless.

"It is the finest instrument I have ever made," Reyanult said gravely. "When Adger told me you were a true musician I had to hear it myself. Even if death were the cost I would pay it gladly. There is no greater reward for an instrument maker than to hear true and good music come from what he has made."

Gingerly, Alistair put the flute to his lips. He reached deep for the Song of the Dawn, the most wonderful he knew, and let it burst through him. A soft and pure sound flowed effortlessly through the silver instrument. The sounds of the song echoed through the flute, if imperfectly, though beautiful in itself. Enchanting music filled not only the little cell, but the whole dungeon with a secret and inexpressible rapture.

Reyanault listened with his eyes closed. Silent tears streamed down his face as he swayed, caught up in the power of the music. For several minutes Alistair played until he felt he could play no more. Abruptly the cell fell silent as Alistair put the flute down.

"Thank you," Reynault whispered. He stepped up to Alistair and kissed his cheek, then turned and left the cell.

"Perhaps the Song will see you out of this prison," Adger said as he hugged the men goodbye. "If it is so willed, then find me again."

"Thank you for this," Alistair said, holding up the flute. "You have no idea what this means."

"I do know," Adger said, his face showing the gravity that takes over men when they speak of something sacred. "I know exactly what it means."

He pulled up his hood and hurried out of the dungeon.

From that moment things began to change quickly in Rabon's dungeon. Alistair played on the silver flute and music brought light into the prison.

One day, a new guard stalked the halls. He yelled for the music to stop, but Alistair didn't stop playing. Instead he listened deep into the guard's heart and heard the song meant to be there. He played the Song of the Blacksmith and the guard ran out of the dungeon.

They never saw him again.

Many new guards began to circulate through the dungeon. Most of the old ones never returned. It was said that they left their posts, refusing to be dungeon guards one day though no one knew what became of them.

It started to become a regular occurrence. A new guard would arrive, and within a week he would be gone, replaced by someone else. One day a new set of guards came down with cloth wrapped around their ears. It didn't seem to help.

Within a week they were gone also, replaced again by more new guards.

Then visitors started to arrive. At first one or two important men, courtiers who had payed handsomely to sneak into the dungeon and hear Alistair play. He would comply with all these requests. Sometimes he would play whatever music came into his heart. At other times he would listen into the hearts of the men who came and play the music that lay buried deep within them. Every so often a coin would be tossed into his cell with a grateful thanks. Many times the hearers would run from the dungeon in tears. Some people returned regularly, and more than a few became friends with the two prisoners. Eventually, word spread about this wonderful musician and folks from all around began to risk their safety and freedom to hear him play.

After he played Alistair would talk with those he had befriended. They told him of the news above the dungeon, about the goings on in the land under Rabon's dominion.

Rabon's grip on the land was weakening, all due to Alistair and his music. They told Alistair of Rabon losing control of the guards, unable to keep any down in the dungeons to guard him. As word spread some of the courtiers began to abandon the court and some even stood up to oppose Rabon's rule. The first few were quickly executed, but the seed had been planted and discontent stirred far and wide. Word passed through the cities, then through the country of this amazing singer and how he was defeating the power of Rabon from down inside a dungeon.

The people grew more bold, and distant places began to defy Rabon's orders. Even in his own castle the great lord was losing his grip on power. The most damaging to Rabon's authority was that he refused to go to the dungeon and confront Alistair himself. When the guards first began to leave it had been suggested that Rabon go down and handle the problem himself. But he refused and seethed with anger at anyone who suggested it. Everyone could see that he feared Alistair, and once he showed fear his power began to unravel.

Alistair always asked after Bella, and he was told she too was being held prisoner. She was confined to one room in the castle and allowed to see no one but Rabon himself and one servant to bring her food and drink. But word leaked out about her and it finally filtered down to Alistair that her health and color were returning, and everyday she looked more like the Bella she had always been.

For several months this situation continued, until one day Bella herself came down to the dungeon. She pulled open the door, lighting her way with the lamp that Alistair had returned, and stepped into his cell without ceremony. Alistair leapt up to embrace her. She allowed herself to be swept into his arms and wept as he hugged her tight.

"Oh Bella, I have dreamed of seeing you again," he told her. "You almost make this dreary place wonderful just with your presence. How did you get out?"

"Rabon allowed me to leave in order to deliver a message to you," Bella said gravely. "He says that you must stop playing your music or he will kill me. If you agree, you and I may have a room in the castle together, and though we will be restricted to that room and a private garden, he will feed us and shelter us as long as we live. But only on the condition that you will never play or sing again. You must give him your instrument and swear never to sing or hum or make any attempt at music. Do this and we can have a life together. If you do not, he will have me beheaded tomorrow morning."

An impossible grief overwhelmed Alistair. Although he could not allow any harm to come to Bella, he also couldn't imagine not singing again either. He had a duty to the Singer and the Eternal Song to play and sing and fill the world with music. And yet, Bella, how could he allow her to die? He wept because he knew what decision he had to make.

"I cannot stop playing," he told Bella in tears. "I would be dead and the world around me suffer if I were to no longer play the music that has been set in my heart."

Bella nodded gravely. Fresh tears filled her eyes but she did not look with hate at Alistair.

"Then play me a song before I must die," she asked softly.

Alistair agreed and took up his flute. He listened into Bella's heart and heard the song that flowed deep within her. It was a mellow and wonderful song, one of the loveliest Alistair had ever heard. As he played, he loved her even more, knowing that of all songs on the hearts of women, he loved this one the best. His heart broke as he played, and he played Song of Grief.

For several hours Alistair played for Bella. She brightened and smiled, and when he was done she kissed him deep and passionately. Alistair heard a new song play on her lips and he grieved that he would not get to hear it again.

"Swear to me you will never stop playing," Bella told him. "Swear that this song will continue until it fills the land."

"I swear it," Alistair told her.

"Then come," Bella told him. "Rabon said that if you refused his offer then you must face him on the hill outside of town. There, one of you will die and the other conquer."

"Then why threaten you with death?" Alistair asked surprised. "Does he intend to kill you?"

"He wants me to hate you," Bella answered with her head down. "He told me you would choose the Song not only over a life with me, but at the cost of my life."

Alistair didn't know what to say. He couldn't look at her any more than she could look at him.

"I'm sorry," he said. "But I owe everything to the Song and I cannot disobey, even at the cost of my own life or any other."

"Do you hate me?"

"Only for a moment," she answered. "Once I heard the music I understood. Much hangs in the balance in our world and whatever it is that you play seems to make all the difference. I'm afraid for you now that you must face Rabon. Just promise me you will always play."

"Don't fear," Alistair tried to reassure her. "Even if I were to fall to Rabon the Song will find a way to return. It moves all things, us as well as the earth itself. To obey is to be a part of the Song, and as long as you dance to what plays in you there is nothing wrong that can harm you."

Bella smiled and took his hand. Together with Railing they walked out of the dungeon and up into the castle above.

* * *

The castle was deserted. No people milled about the courtyard, the throne room had fallen silent, all the halls were empty. In a storage room they found Railing's spear and bow. The hunter happily rearmed himself and continued with his friends.

After they had searched through the castle, the three left and made their way out of the city. The sun was setting when they reached the grassy hill. A circle of old stones lay half tumbled and wearing away atop the hill. Rabon waited in the midst of them, surrounded by magic circles and symbols he had traced in chalk and a litter of potions and instruments that was part of his dark trade. He was clad in purple robes, covered in symbols written in gold.

"Behold your fate, Singer," Rabon hissed as he swayed in the incense smoke that rolled from golden censers. "Today you learn real power."

Fire flew from Rabon's fingertips. The flames curled around his hand and circled around him before he thrust it towards Alistair.

With only his silver flute to defend himself Alistair took up his instrument and played the Song of Fire. The flames immediately fell and burned harmlessly out on the green hill.

Rabon's eyes went wide with shock. Quickly, he recovered and summoned a grey cloud and sent it towards Alistair. Alistair played the Song of the Wind and the cloud blew away.

For hours into the darkness the fight went on. Rabon summoned lightning and Alistair stilled it with the Song of the Storm. The earth shook and was calmed by the Song of the Earth. Demons were summoned and creatures from dark places called up. Alistair listened to the stars singing and played what they cried out. Not a single beast of the dark could stand that sound and fled beneath its power.

From around Rabon grew a dark cloud that crackled with green and blue sparks of electricity. Out of the cloud, the magician threw a foul array of strange power. They were all countered by the songs, rendered impotent by the music that Alistair played faithfully, almost in a trance as the power flowed through him.

All night long the men warred this way. Nothing that Rabon summoned could touch Alistair. The cloud of darkness pulsed around him with evil intent, obeying the whims of its master, crackling with energy.

The sun rose and the attacks on Alistair slowed down. He saw Rabon breathing heavy and soaked in sweat, the exhaustion clear on the sorcerer's face. Alistair, empowered by the dawn and more full of energy than when he began, turned his music towards Rabon.

He played the Song of the Dawn, and the dark cloud around Rabon shuddered but did not fail. Rabon laughed as Alistair played, in full knowledge that the song had no power over him and could do him no harm.

"You see we are at a standstill," Rabon breathed with effort. "There is no magic of mine that can harm you, and your pitiful songs have no effect on me. Let us make a truce. I will give you half of my kingdom and you will leave me alone and I will not hinder or harass you. If you will but promise to keep your song out of my domain, then I will not harm your people.

"What say you? We cannot harm each other let us then live in peace with one another."

Alistair paused and considered Rabon's proposal. Perhaps, he thought, this was a reasonable truce to this conflict. He imagined himself setting up his own kingdom. Perhaps over time he would attract all the people to his land. It would be peaceful and prosperous and a light to the whole world. He would teach others to sing as the ruler and he would dispense justice wisely.

As Alistair thought about these things the song within him faltered. He felt it fade with disappointment at even the thought of peace with Rabon. The lord sensed that something weakened in Alistair and he lashed out with suddenly renewed violence.

Quickly Alistair renewed his song. He played the first one that came into his head, the Song of the Wind. Rabon's power receded as the song resumed and a wind nearly the power of a gale rose up and battered the men on the hilltop. But as before, the dark was not vanquished.

The black cloud still swirled around Rabon. It crackled with its strange power and pulsed in a fog about its master. For the moment it did not grow, but was not touched by the songs that Alistair played.

Rabon smiled again at Alistair's frustration, at the impotence of the song to destroy his power. An evil laugh, full of all the malice that festered in his heart, came groaning out of Rabon's mouth. The laugh was joyless, fueled only by the particular spite of one who, though he cannot win, has denied victory to another.

Alistair listened to the wicked laugh and shuddered, amazed that such a dark sound could issue from a human heart. He heard in it all the hatred for life, the pleasure for suffering, the thirst to destroy all that was beautiful, the reckless lust for power, the love of lies, and almost a joy, though it was a joyless joy, in seeing all that was wrong subvert what was right. He could hear wrongness, as clear as if it were a song unto itself. Perversion, deep and twisted, echoed in that laugh, and Alistair feared that if he stopped playing for a moment it would infect and twist him too.

But there was something else he heard. Beneath all the wrongness and hate and decay he thought he detected another sound. So he listened deeper.

Beneath all the layers of wickedness he heard fear. Alistair knew instantly this was what drove Rabon. He heard the fear of the dark, of unknown things, the fear of the simple power that normal people carried in their hearts, the fear of being overwhelmed by the world, of being carried away by the hapless stream of life that cared nothing for one man and his destiny. But most of all there was fear of a dark thing that stalked the shadows and thirsted to feed on his flesh and soul. It was a fear of the demon Enlil.

Yet there was a sound beneath even the fear.

Alistair listened deeper and heard the sound of disappointment. He heard of a young man striving to find freedom and peace but only hearing reproach and discouragement. He heard the hatred and fear others cast at him because of his lineage and power. He heard insults and lies and shouts of fear and threats that hardened the heart of a young man who wanted to embrace the world almost as much as he wanted the world to embrace him. But all he heard was disappointment.

Still Alistair listened deeper.

He heard the sounds of a boy crying. He heard the boy haunted by dark forces that only he could see, wraiths and shadows that traced the corners of the night and whispered strange things that chased away the happiness of the sun. He could hear the boy, longing only for his father to embrace him, to assure him of his love. Yet all he got were lessons in magic and puffs of smoke and strange characters drawn in chalk to keep the dark figures at bay. He could hear the longing in the boy, the need for warmth that was the only thing he desired, and in truth, was all that could banish the fear of the night. But the poor father knew nothing of the affection that children crave. So the father only sought to banish the shadows, even as he knew he could not banish the whisperings of Enlil, those dark mutterings that frightened the boy above all.

Still, Alistair listened deeper.

He heard at last happiness, dim though the sound was. It was the happiness of the very young. It was the happiness of innocence. He heard the happiness that loves to play with the sunlight and run beneath the flight of the bird. He heard the happiness that sees wonders everywhere, especially in the commonplace and everyday, the things that we drag our children by, for we have lost that true sight and are blind to their splendors. He heard the brief time when Rabon played with the world.

Still, Alistair listened deeper.

There at last, past the corruption and the fear and the disappointment and longing, even past the happiness, underneath all the twistedness and perversion and lust to destroy all that was beautiful, silent as a whisper and clinging to life, Alistair heard the song.

He heard the Song of Rabon.

Like all true songs, this was not the Song of the Self, the songs that men create to make their own life. This was part of the Eternal Song, the true song. It was the song that was sung into Rabon's heart as soon as he came into being, the song of his true destiny, of the man he was meant to be. It was the song of a philosopher and seer, one who counseled men with gentleness and compassion because he could see all the dark and malevolent things that tempted and twisted men and sought to undo them. It was the song of one who could walk the rim of this world and the other, and in doing so bring light into the hearts of man. It was a song like few others, yet in this form it was unique, as all true songs are.

But the song was dying. It was so dim that Alistair could barely hear it struggle to breathe out life. No longer could it try to sway Rabon any more, for it could barely live and wait for someone to hear and bring it back to life again.

Alistair listened. He let the song capture him. Then he played the Song of Rabon.

As soon as the first notes issued from the flute the magician cried out and fell to the ground. A blood-curling scream tore from Rabon's mouth. He covered his ears and doubled over, hurling obscenities and curses at Alistair.

The dark cloud around Rabon shuddered and died. It blew away on the breeze and took with it the lightning and the fire, leaving Rabon defenseless. The magician could do nothing but writhe on the ground in agony.

Rabon tried to shut out the sounds of the awful song. But as soon as Alistair played, the song within his heart heard it and leapt to life, rejoicing and pulsing with light. Rabon cried and screamed, hating the song he heard with his ears and hating even more the song that swirled inside him.

"STOP!!! STOP!!! WHY DO YOU TORTURE ME WITH THIS MISERY!!!" Rabon screamed out. "STOP OH PLEASE STOOOOOP!!!"

Rabon cried out and Alistair played all the louder. As the song in Rabon grew the song grew in Alistair's music, and both their power increased. Rabon wept as the songs played all around him, finally convulsing in agony, tortured by the sounds.

Suddenly, the magician stood up. He reached for some colored sand and threw it into the magic circle drawn behind him.

"*Conjuritas Maleficorum Abjura Enlil Deporta Te!*" Rabon yelled as he threw the sand.

A rush of flame flew up from the magic circle as the sand hit the writings. The earth opened up in fire and a winged beast rose up from the depths. It spread its leathery wings wide and uncovered a grotesque body covered in scales and smiled through red eyes and venomous teeth.

"Who dares to summon Enlil little worm?" the demon hissed. "Ah, Rabon, of all men I would expect you last to call upon me. You know how I hunger for your flesh."

"Make it stop," Rabon wept. "Make this music stop and I will let you have a portion."

The demon grimaced, noticing the song for the first time. It bared its teeth and growled towards Alistair. Though Alistair trembled inside he played on, fearful that the music was all that protected him.

"I have no power over that music," Enlil uttered hatefully. "It is that sound which my lord's kingdom wars against forever. I would wipe it away from the earth if I could."

"Can even you not give me relief from this music?" Rabon cried out desperately. "I must have it to an end."

"In my lord's kingdom there is no music," the demon smiled. "I will take you there, but know I will devour you."

Rabon looked back at Alistair, still playing the song that was in Rabon's heart. Fresh tears fell from his eyes and flowed down his cheeks. He dropped his head and cried aloud, torn with indecision.

"Rabon don't!" Bella cried out surprising everyone with a sudden show of concern. "Don't be a fool!"

"Why do you care?" Rabon spat at her. "You have no

care for me!"

"But this is madness," Bella plead. "No man should give himself to that thing."

"I have no choice," Rabon answered with his head hung low. "That music will kill me."

"But it will give you life, real life."

Rabon breathed deeply and stood up. He turned around and faced the demon glaring hideously down on him. Nothing but hate glared from its reptilian eyes, yet Rabon took a step towards it until he stood on the edge of the pit.

"I choose death over that hateful song," he said. "Enlil, take me."

"Say the words!" the demon hissed with barely restrained hunger. "Say them!"

"I give myself to thee," Rabon pledged solemnly. "Body, mind and spirit I am yours. I give myself to thee. Heart and spirit I pledge it freely. I give myself to thee."

With a roar Enlil reached out and plucked Rabon up in a clawed grasp. The magician cried out in sudden fear, perhaps at last realizing what he had given himself to. With his screams of terror echoing on the new day the demon plunged down into the earth, taking a flailing Rabon with him. The hole closed up and silence fell upon the hill.

As soon as the earth closed up Alistair stopped playing. Exhaustion washed over him, a tiredness deep and complete. He stumbled and fell towards the ground. The last thing he heard was Bella cry out to him and Railing running over to his side before he lost consciousness.

Railing and Bella took Alistair back to the castle, which still lay deserted. He slept for the better part of two days. As he slept, he was tortured with dreams of Rabon being taken into the bowels of the earth. Over and over again he saw the scene of mad desperation. And every time he saw it, he wept for the life lost.

News of Rabon's defeat spread quickly through the land. Men came tentatively to the castle to see their new lord. When Alistair told them he was not a lord, but a musician, the people begged him to rule over them.

Alistair considered, but only for a moment. He heard the song of his own heart, and it was the song of a singer, not a ruler. He told the people they would have to find a ruler of their own. After several weeks of confusion they finally assembled a council of elders that met at the castle. At first, they gathered to decide what sort of government they should have. They ended up deciding to rule themselves after swearing and committing to paper an oath vowing never to let the tyranny that Rabon perpetrated upon them to ever happen again.

The castle became a center for the new leadership, lived in by no one and visited freely by all. Alistair would play there often, but more likely he would be found roaming far and wide with Bella and Railing, playing to all who would hear. He and Bella married after a time and enjoyed the adventure of life together while guiding the land in the best way they knew how.

After a few months traveling with Bella and Alistair, a new longing took over Railing's heart. One night he rose, stirred awake by the sound of the moon, and looked out over the plain bathed in the beauty of the night. He looked up at the stars and sky, at the pale moonlight filtering down to the earth, and he felt a stirring in his heart, or rather a remembrance.

In his heart he was a hunter, and he longed to hunt again. Except this longing was a particular sort of hunt, one that he had begun but never finished. That morning, he bade farewell to Alistair and Bella, mounted upon his destrier and departed with their blessing.

For many days Railing rode, searching for the trail of the Hunter King's herd. It took much travail and searching, as a quest of this magnitude must, but one day at dusk he spied the unmistakable traces of Alvalon's favored ones. He stayed upon the trail hard until he found them beneath the crest of a hill, grazing without concern.

Railing plunged into the herd, this time not even bothering to raise a weapon. He knew he could not slay one of these noble animals. He rode until he saw the white doe, graceful and beautiful beyond all the other creatures.

The hunter's awen overcame him and Railing gave chase as the doe fled. Deep into the forest they rode, hunter and hunted, both running and chasing for joy of the hunt. Railing eventually found what he wanted, and he laid down with Nivena one night and his happiness became more complete. She chose him as her own and he became, by right, the Hunter King himself.

Many years would pass until Railing and Alistair met again. Their reunion was not an altogether happy occasion, as the land was once again in peril. But that is a tale for another day.

As for Alistair, he passed by the city of his origin quite regularly as he and Bella traveled the land. He could not help but gaze at the cold, steel walls with a mixture of sadness and indecision when he did. He knew there was something he should be doing concerning the city, but he did not know what.

Alistair knew the citizens of the city should be free. They should live in the wonderful places he had discovered and come to love, to hear the songs of life, that if they only knew what the outside world had to offer, they would gladly flee the city. But he also remembered Rabon, how he chose death over life and thought that many may not want to be free. After all, he and Railing were the only ones that ever sought freedom. But what if there were more, he also asked himself, men like him who wanted something but did not know what.

For many months Alistair tortured himself with

questions like these, debating what to do with the city. Bella could see the conflict on his face and one day she asked him about it.

"Do you want to go back to the city?" she asked him.

Alistair shook his head and looked to the ground.

"I want to free them," he said. "At least give them an opportunity for true freedom. But I'm afraid that they do not want it. Like Rabon, they will choose death over life."

"All you can do is give them the choice," Bella observed. "Some will love you and love the Song, others won't. Present your case and let them choose."

"How can I give them the choice," Alistair sighed. "It is a place designed to destroy wonder. It is full of lights and distraction. Why a person can't even see...."

Alistair trailed off at that last thought, suddenly energized by a powerful idea. Like Bella had suggested, he would give them a choice. He simply had to show them the options they had.

He had to show them wonder.

It took him a few days to plan, and he didn't even know it would work. He chose his songs carefully and with trepidation. He had never used songs in this way, and he hoped that they would obey him for this particular task.

It took several trips around the outskirts of the wall to find what he needed. Eventually he found it, the massive tangle of wires and tubes and towering machinery that hugged the outside of the wall. An incessant hum, almost a growl came from the machines as they fed electricity into the city. Alistair was sure they were the generators. He could almost tell by the sound they made, as if they were a distorted song themselves, all grinds and turbines turning, producing perpetual false power.

He waited until night, for Alistair knew it would not work during the day. A sliver of moon rose up at dusk and the stars were immediately blotted out by the mass of ugly, weak light that blazed from the city. Even outside the walls the stars could barely be seen. Alistair remembered seeing them for the first time and he knew what he was doing was right.

Placing the flute to his lips, Alistair began to play. He played a Song of the Vines, a song of growth that reached in and covered the generator and filled it with green life. When the generator was covered inside and out with growth he could hear it hum louder, working hard to keep up the pace as plants grew inside and out.

The generator still worked and Alistair knew he would need something stronger. He listened to what lay beneath the generator, what life might be stirring beneath the massive machine.

Almost immediately he heard it. Twisting roots that had snaked beneath the generator long ago still waited to burst through the concrete and steel. So Alistair played the Song of the Oak, and they began to grow.

The roots grew thicker and longer, they bunched up beneath the concrete floor of the machine and butted into stone and rock and steel. But Alistair played on and the oak roots were powered by the song.

Alistair played a Song of Life and the roots grew stronger. He mixed a variation with the Song of the Oak, playing a new song and the roots inched into the concrete, doing the work of twenty years in the space of an hour. Eventually they broke through, and saplings appeared in the floor of the generator.

At first they were cut off by the whir and spin of the machines. But they grew thicker and stronger, filling the generator with branches of green and vibrant life. Outside Alistair could hear the hum of the machines grow to a whine. Metal clanged and smoke flowed out. The generator began to tremble.

Eventually, no matter how powerful a machine may be, it

cannot overcome the power of life. Life flows from a place that we yet know not of, a place full of mysterious and deep power. And though it flows in us we are not masters of it. This is the power that turns the planet and fuels the scorching fire of the sun and draws the ocean to ebb and flow. Who are we to stand up to that? What are our petty machines to reckon with such a force? Our machines may destroy us, but they will never destroy life.

Even the mighty generator had to relent to the oaks. The trees, fueled by the Song of Life filled and grew, taller and thicker. They filled every corner of the machine and pushed against it with the strength of the earth, and even the strength that lies behind the earth.

The generator shuddered and whined, and with an anti-climatic ping, it fell silent.

The lights inside the city died and the sky sprang to life. A silence fell over the population all at once. Something had happened that had never happened before. Fear gripped every single citizen that found themselves in darkness for the first time.

Outside Alistair heard the collective silence, then the gasps. Some cried in fear and terror, others exclaimed in wonder. Almost immediately the city was abuzz with life, perhaps for the first time in generations. They all saw something they had never seen before. Above their heads blazed a thousand lights, filling the darkness with their glory and their song.

For the first time, the people saw the stars.

CPSIA information can be obtained at www.ICGtesting.com
Printed in the USA
LVOW10s0339100214

373008LV00002B/4/P